ROGUE

D.J. Gelner

Orion's Comet

To the universe and random chance, for allowing us to make it
this far.

ONE

July 20, 2066
T-Minus 9 hours, 32 minutes

Joe Grissom thrummed his dark brown fingers on the eggshell-colored armrest.

He checked his watch.

12:28.

Wyatt was late.

He looked around the room, desperate to take his mind off of the unappealing task at hand. What had once been a methodically-assembled, thoroughly modern apartment now appeared faded and worn. It always seemed like the 3D-printed stuff didn't last as long as hand-crafted materials, though for many peoples' sakes, he certainly hoped that wasn't to be the case in just a few short hours.

Now that he thought about it, the whole hallway looked *wrong* on his way over. The glass no longer shimmered in the moonlight, and the brushed metal was beginning to collect dingy fingerprints, marring the otherwise sparkling finish to which he was accustomed.

He snorted. None of it would matter soon enough.

Muffled sounds from the other side of the door eventually morphed into loud, boisterous singing as the door swung open.

"I am a man, a...*space*-going man!" a tall, lanky fellow with a prominent nose and mane of sandy-blonde hair belted out the words with a flourish. He reached for the light switch and flicked it on as the door shut itself behind him with a "thud."

Wyatt's eyes went wide, ""H...Hey Joe. What's up?"

Joe steeled his nerves, "'Evenin', Wyatt," he unfolded himself out of the chair and rose to his full, impressive height. "He's not happy," Joe's voice was deep and gravely, though simultaneously soft and eroded by years of dust and grit.

Wyatt mustered as much bravado as he could through shrugged, quaking shoulders.

"Well, maybe I'm not, either."

"You messed up," Joe's eyes narrowed.

"Messed up?! I never had a chance! I was set up from the start," Wyatt's eyes darted back to the door behind him. He reached for the knob but the handle failed to yield. He turned and focused on the brushed metal tube hanging from Joe's belt. Though the two small prongs on its end were lifeless, the implications of its very presence were all too clear. "Y...you lift that off'a grey shirt? Or—oh my God. He *got* you! I never thought I'd see the day. Joe Grissom working for—"

2

Joe's neck bulged as his jaw jutted out, "I'm not proud of it. Man's gotta' do what a man's gotta' do."

Wyatt took several cautious steps toward him, "That's the *point*, Joe! Don't you see? Hasn't he *told* you?"

Joe's hand moved toward the cylinder that hung from his belt, "He told me enough. Told me what you did."

A couple more steps. Wyatt lifted a weak wave toward Joe, "Oh, come on now, that's all *b.s.*"

"Is it?" Joe raised an eyebrow.

"Ya' gotta'…ya' gotta' *ask* yer'self, Joe—" Wyatt tried in vain to not slur the words, "Whass' in it for *him*? If he's so 'powerful' and 'connected,' why are *you* the one jumping through all of these hoops for the *possibility* that tomorrow, you're gonna' get to go on that—" Wyatt nodded at the gigantic structure outside of the window before he squinted, "Oh my God…what's going on over at the ship?"

Joe turned his head to follow, which gave Wyatt the opening he sought. The tipsy man bent his shaky knees and leapt at Joe, belt level.

Joe cursed his gullibility as Wyatt connected with his legs. He reeled for several moments before, mid-air, he reached out a meaty paw to slap away Wyatt's hand, which lunged for the metal cylinder.

"CRACK"

Joe's head connected with the flat side of the couch. He screamed with pain, a booming, primal yell as Wyatt struggled to assert every one of his lean muscle fibers over this man nearly twice his size.

Joe locked eyes with the man as he fought through the dull pain forming at the back of his head. Wyatt's formerly placid blue eyes had gone wild and red. His jaws gnashed as he searched for some weakness, some way to get at the implement hanging at Joe's side.

Before Joe could react, Wyatt was upon him, trying to sink his teeth into Joe's neck.

Joe gritted through the pain. He cursed himself, if only because he wished he had thought of the maneuver first.

Joe raised an elbow at the fiend. The joint connected with the satisfying sound and sensation of bone cracking across bone.

Wyatt reeled from the force of the blow. Joe snarled as he rose first to a three-point stance, then into a crouch. He reached to his thigh and gripped the cool metal form of the stinger stick firmly in his hand. He didn't even bother unbuttoning the clasp as he yanked on the device and it came free. He pressed the large blue button on the side of the implement. Immediately the cylinder lengthened as the two prongs hissed to life with an awful whine followed by a dull hiss.

A hiss that Joe and Wyatt knew too well.

"No…God *no*, Joe!" Wyatt scooted backward on the seat of his pants. "After all I've—*we've*—been through, you can't just—"

Joe brought the hissing rod down onto Wyatt's shoulder, quickly and coldly. As the prongs connected with their target, a violent noise swelled, like a muffled electronic trumpet resonating around the room's cozy confines.

Wyatt's body seized and bounced on the floor. His eyes rolled back in his head and an unpleasant gurgling sound forced its way out through the bubbling saliva on his lips.

Joe made himself watch, to see what this madness had driven him to. There was a point far in his past when he would've thought of some other way, a more *honorable* way, to get what he so desperately needed:

More time.

Sadly for everyone in the entire complex, there was none.

Or at least any more time as they once knew it.

He caught the first whiff of burning flesh as he brought the horrible weapon away from Wyatt's still-twitching body. He pulled out a syringe filled with dark blue liquid.

Joe took a deep breath before he plunged the syringe into Wyatt's back.

Wyatt stopped seizing and took in two deep, sucking lungfuls of air. A thin howl shattered the silence in the room and sent a chill down Joe's spine. He covered his ears and shut his eyes, desperate to drown out the banshee-like cries.

Then it stopped; Wyatt dropped to the floor, his body completely motionless.

Joe wrenched one eye open, then the other. His heart still raced as he gasped to catch his breath. As the adrenaline drained from his brain, his muscles took on their dull, familiar ache as he propped himself up into a crouch.

He eyed Wyatt's still frame splayed out on the ground.

"*That's* what you get for *biting me!*" Joe yelled as he rose to his feet. He gave Wyatt a swift kick in the ribs, though there was no way his friend felt it. He quickly removed a syringe from his pocket and drove it into one of the veins that slowly rose to the surface on Wyatt's exposed forearms. He pulled on the plunger, filling the reservoir of the syringe with dark, thick blood.

Joe capped the needle and placed it in his pocket. He patted the damp spot on his neck as he fought through heaving breaths and brought his blood-slicked fingers to his eyes.

He mumbled a curse word and took several long steps over to the sink outside of the bathroom. Joe's hands were too big for the faucet handles, but he had long ago perfected the art of moving the handle with the rough, calloused part of his palm.

Joe's forearms prickled with goosebumps as the cold water washed over his hands. It was a good five seconds before he even looked at his reflection.

It was almost as if the figure in the mirror had punched him.

His eyes were sunken and hollow, like a couple of marbles plopped into soft mud. Blood streaked over his dark face like warpaint.

Joe pooled some water in his hands and brought it to his cheeks. He dug his palms into his rough, muck-blasted skin.

Had he aged so much in the past three years?

Worse still, Joe knew the answer immediately:

It doesn't matter.

He shook his head and held his own gaze. What bothered him most wasn't the awful deed he had just committed, or his reasons for committing it.

It was the lack of remorse staring back at him.

Joe made his way over to Wyatt and kneeled beside him. He smiled thinly and shook his head; though he had been caught up in the heat of the moment, it still didn't make what he had done any more *right*. He reached in his pocket, searching only briefly before he found what he was looking for. He placed a large hand in Wyatt's shirt pocket before he removed it and patted the object he had placed there through the heavy linen fabric.

"That's for you, bud," Joe said. "I'll get ya' back someday."

He collected the rod and reattached it to his belt before he keyed in a new code to the door. The door opened with a satisfying "whoosh" as the cool air blew across Joe's still-damp face.

One stop to go… he thought. He looked upward in contemplation.

He checked both ways before he moved swiftly along the sides of the now-dull facility walls, another shadow in a complex full of them.

TWO

Three Years Earlier

Joe brought his hands away from his brow. He wrung out his thin handkerchief and put it in his back pocket. The trickle of discarded sweat evaporated soon after it hit the dry, cracked desert floor beneath him.

He reached for his belt and found a set of long, spindly fingers still attached to one of the denim loops.

"Can I let go now, dad?" Even under the circumstances, Joe detected the faintest amount of contempt in the boy's voice, as if he could barely comprehend what exactly was at stake.

'Guess that makes two of us, Joe thought.

He blew out a bemused smile and nodded as he took his son's hand once more. One step. Another. Over and over again. The hot spots on his feet grew larger and more bothersome with each one, but he dared not stop.

As if to punctuate the thought, a couple of men twenty feet in front of them shoved and yelled at one another. The crowd dispersed around them, terrified that they would somehow be implicated in the brouhaha.

The shriek of a whistle broke the commotion as the grey shirts descended upon the two men, arms raised, clutching the brushed metal rods that whined with electricity.

One of the grey shirts was a red-faced cuss of a man with a matching, silver buzz cut that shone in the unforgiving sun and a hundred dollar grin on his face. He stifled a laugh as he brought the futuristic club down on both men repeatedly, through the gurgling noise until they lay on the ground, motionless. The grey shirts signaled their counterparts over the fence, and hauled the two over the barbed wire.

"Where do those men go, Da—"

Before the boy could finish the question, two gunshots rang out, sharp and true through the clear desert air.

Several children cried, startled by the noise. Their parents shot them daggers as they continued to shuffle along through the caked, cracked mud.

Joe shook his head again, "Don't step out of line, Mason. Understand?"

Mason nodded.

Joe raised an eyebrow, the question implicit:

Really?

Mason bobbed his head.

"I understand, dad."

"Good."

"Two fewer to worry about," a voice said over Joe's shoulder.

He turned without stopping to find a gangly man with wild blonde hair flashing him a grin.

Joe merely nodded, "I ain't in the mood for trouble, friend."

The man shrugged, "Just makin' conversation. Kind'a boring for us loners out here walkin' through the damned desert."

Joe looked forward and re-gripped Mason's hand, hoping the man would move on to someone else.

Instead, he caught an outstretched hand in his peripheral vision.

"Name's Wyatt. Wyatt Port," he said.

Joe thought for a moment before he snorted and brusquely took the man's hand in his own.

"Joe."

Wyatt smiled before he furrowed his brow, "Joe?" He paused in thought, "Joe…Joe *Grissom?*"

Joe stifled a thin grin.

"Yeah," he affected a sigh, as if weary of being recognized so often.

Wyatt's eyes went wide, "Oh man, are you *serious?* This is *awesome!* I'm one'a the biggest S.C. football fans around, more Trojan than Hector himself. I'll be *damned* if you weren't the best linebacker to ever come outta' there. Better than Seau!"

Joe snorted, "I don't know about that." He looked down, and was secretly happy that Mason had turned his attention to the lanky stranger.

Wyatt shook his head, "Man, what happened—?"

"In the pros? Guess I just couldn't hack it."

Joe waited a while for the usual follow-up, one that every slack-jawed yokel never thought twice about asking.

It never came.

Wyatt changed the subject, "So, guess you all got roped into this business too, huh?"

Joe shrugged, "What other choice did we have?"

"I dunno. A lotta' talk 'bout it bein' a big hoax and everything. Just a way for the government to lock up a bunch'a folks, throw away the key."

"I highly doubt that," Joe's gaze never wavered from the mass of people in front of him.

One foot.

The other.

"What? You don't think the government's in the business'a lyin' to folks?"

Joe shook his head, "Not about somethin' like this. Not an operation of this size. Just doesn't make sense."

"S'pose you're right…" Wyatt tailed off. "You have to admit, though, it is pretty re-damned-diculous, don't ya' think? It's the lottery to end all lotteries. What're the odds that—"

Joe looked over his shoulder and bobbed his head, "Better than the odds out there."

11

Wyatt paused and followed Joe's gaze, even as Joe and Mason trudged onward. He shook his head at the thought before he jogged a few steps to catch up with the former USC linebacker. Wyatt looked down at Mason before he whispered, "What if it misses?"

Joe stopped for a moment, just an instant as the sweat poured off his brow. He looked at Wyatt, skin already reddening from the hot Nevada sun, and leveled dark, ominous eyes at this new pest.

"Ain't. Gonna'. Miss." Joe said through clenched teeth. He looked down at Mason, whose scrunched eyes confirmed that he hadn't heard the men.

Joe continued on his way.

One foot.

The other.

Wyatt stood and contemplated the man's statement, its full implications before he continued on, some ways behind.

Just how far are we going to have to walk? Joe thought. It had been hours since they had been asked to surrender their cars. Joe wondered where the automobiles went as the grey shirts drove them off, two-by-two, down the narrow road and over the horizon, the most orderly traffic jam that Joe had ever seen.

The leather of his sole frayed and started to dig into the ball of his foot, but Joe didn't dare so much as let his lip quiver.

One foot.

The other.

Again. And again.

Occasionally, a sign made out of thin sheet metal would pop out of the desert landscape, usually pocked with buckshot holes left by bored teenagers years before. Though the white background had long ago scraped and faded, the large, dark green numbers were still legible, as was the smaller type underneath, "U.S. Government Property, Keep Out. Violators Will Be Prosecuted."

The last of these signs, which was numbered "26," was curiously well-maintained, as if it had been replaced just for this long march through the desert.

Another half hour passed in silence before their pace slowed and stopped in front of hundreds of archways that housed ramps down to tunnels, each one a yawning, stainless steel mouth waiting to selectively sample those deemed worthy to enter.

Next to each opening was what looked to be a processing station, manned by a grey shirt holding a curious device with a straw-like appendage attached to it, the end of which was replaced after every person processed. Above the grey shirt was a holomonitor that occasionally flashed green or red, in between a montage of smiling, multicultural faces and the letters "SSC."

They were only a few people from the front of the line. A pitiable-looking fiftiesh man with a scraggly beard and flabby arms sucked in his gut and puffed out his chest.

The grey shirt at the front of the line shouted, "Remember, everyone, we want to accept as many of you as possible, but for obvious reasons, not everyone will be able to continue on." His mustached lip quivered with revulsion as he turned back to the greasy little man and placed the straw on his finger.

The screen flashed red.

"Try it again," the greasy man affixed a sheepish grin.

"I'm sorry, sir, if you'll move over here," the grey shirt motioned to a thin paddock to his right.

"No, there must be some mistake—"

The grey shirt sighed and reached for his weapon. He hoped the mere indication would be enough to quiet the man.

Instead, the sad man's protests doubled.

"No...no I'm an academic! I'm one of the foremost scholars on art history in the entire—"

"Then why weren't you on the *List?!*"

The grey shirt's voice rose as he grabbed the long, thin cylinder and swung it at the poor academic's shoulder. The horrible whine reverberated around the tunnel entrance and was spit out at the rest of the waiting masses, simultaneously a wordless warning and a reminder of what all they were giving up.

I wonder if that's the point... Joe thought.

The man doubled over in pain, then fell to his knees.

"Get him outta' here!" the first grey shirt shouted. His two colleagues complied and dragged him through the long, chain-linked paddock next to the processing station, and onto the dusty green buses idling in the desert heat.

Joe felt a tug on his sleeve. He looked down at Mason, barely able to hide his own fear with an arched eyebrow.

"Is that gonna' happen to us, Dad?" His eyes went wide as the corners of his mouth drooped into a frown. Joe still certainly thought of Mason as a boy, but he was already a strapping young lad of thirteen, barely able to go to school for a couple of years before—

If *we make it through here*, Joe thought.

He shook his head, "Of course not." He tried to muster a smile, but was afraid it came off as him choking down something bitter.

He didn't know why he was so worried. After all, Joe of all people should have no problem getting through the checkpoint, and it's not like the boy's mother had been any genetic slouch, either.

Still, the thought gnawed at the back of his mind like a hungry praying mantis.

This is wrong.

They waited their turn until the hippy-dippy, long-haired star child in front of them was red-lighted and carted off to the buses.

Joe nodded at Mason as he squeezed the boy's hand and took a long, lumbering stride forward.

The grey shirt motioned to the tablet he held, outstretched.

Didn't even ask for a name, Joe thought. *The better to keep their distance, cart us off if we fail.*

The grey shirt replaced the end of the straw and stuck it onto Joe's finger.

Joe felt the pinch of the nanoneedle as it entered his skin, not so much painful as an annoyance like a mosquito bite on one's index finger.

Almost immediately, Joe's driver's license picture came up on the guard's tablet, complete with every piece of information publicly available about him, which for Joe included several "Where are They Now?" features from various sports websites.

A rotating yellow circle soon joined the array of data, the sign that the tablet was searching the pre-desert trek database for a match.

Joe bit his lip and shuffled his feet. To steel his gaze, his thought about Madison, and what she had done when she found out what Joe intended to do with their son.

He was so distracted, he hardly noticed the large, bright green light above the grey shirt.

"Wonderful. Congratulations." The grey shirt's bemusement was apparent as he expertly removed the nanoneedle from the end of the straw, discarded it in a large bin, and attached another.

Joe thought it likely that the man was overdue for a break, or had at least been on shift for far too long. He surveyed the crowd behind them, a mass of pathetic, dirt-caked creatures making painfully subdued small talk in the hopes that they wouldn't offend or otherwise garner the ire of the grey shirts.

Not likely to get one anytime soon, Joe thought.

"And now for you," the grey shirt placed the straw on Mason's hand. The teenager looked up at his father, eyebrow raised, skin glistening with sweat.

Joe instinctively placed his hand on his kid's shoulder, forcing him to stay steady. The boy's skin felt cold and clammy despite the desert heat.

The picture of Mason that Joe had e-mailed the Powers That Be popped up, as did most of Mason's vital info, followed by the swirling yellow circle of indecision.

Joe's grip on Mason's shoulder strengthened as the tablet took far longer to process the boy's DNA sequencing than it had his own.

Or at least it seemed as much.

Joe's pupils followed the circle in tight, narrow arcs. Had he been less concerned at the moment, he would've appreciated the irony that even if Mason came up green, even if they both passed, it was a harbinger of what was to come; three years at the mercy of machines and scanners. Cold, judging eyes without an ounce of kindness behind them. No "special cases." No "exceptions."

Just "the rules."

He couldn't take it any more; his upper teeth ground through the flesh of his inner lip against their lower counterparts. He welcomed the salty blood that filled his mouth, and reminded him that he was, in fact, human.

A large rectangle filled the screen as Joe sucked in two large lungfuls of air.

It was green.

He exhaled abruptly and patted his son on the shoulder.

"Wonderful. Congratulations." The grey shirt repeated as his eyes drifted down to the tablet. He produced a device and quickly stuck each of them on the right shoulder, like tagging cattle, before he replaced the nanoneedle, ran a hand through his glistening, thinning hair, and waved the next person forward.

Mason grinned. Gone was the forced teenaged moodiness, the affected air of superiority. His eyes danced with life, surpassed only by his father's own laughing eyes.

Joe wanted to swing the boy up on his shoulders, to twirl him around and dance and celebrate.

Instead, he took another two deep breaths and grabbed his boy's hand as they descended down the ramp and into a tunnel, into their new life.

THREE

July 18, 2064
T-Minus 2 years, 2 days, 15 hours, 2 minutes

"Ca-CHINK!"

The pickaxe easily carved into the formerly unforgiving metal ore.

Joe swung the implement rhythmically, like a metronome slowly chipping away at the hollowed-out cache of raw material, in this case, titanium.

He raised a sleeveless arm to slick away the sweat pouring off of his dark brow. Though they were God-knows-how many feet underground, the unforgiving sun still baked through the tunnels and rocks, and made life in the mines similar to working in a brick oven.

'Least I drew ore-work first, Joe thought.

It was tough, physical labor, but it allowed Joe to think about other things, more pressing things, like where were the laser mining tools he had been promised in the science fiction stories and video games of his youth?

They can make all the "reinforced alloys" they want, but they don't save my back, not a lick, he thought.

Truth be told, the reinforced alloy pick axes made Joe's labor, and that of the dozens of men and women who lined the tunnels, much easier than he could possibly imagine. The graphene-steel blend easily tore through the hard rock like it was the consistency of cold, lumpy mashed potatoes, and not one of the strongest, lightest elements known to man.

It didn't hurt that they were simply cleaning up after the gigantic robots that had carved these tunnels months ago, machines that had long since been unleashed on other swaths of virgin ground to create more holes in the earth to be manned by the seemingly endless tide of human mop-up crews.

Grey-shirted foremen roamed the tunnels, stinger sticks clasped loosely around belt loops for easy access, eager to use them at the slightest disruption of order lest their own futures be placed in jeopardy.

Their scowling faces were contrasted by the scannerbots that glided through the tunnels, each one's single, warm, green eye reassuring and welcoming.

"You're doing great!" one such scannerbot said as it flew past Joe, "Keep up the great work!"

Joe snarled. He plunged the pick axe into the rock again.

Two men down, Danny Hannigan, all five-foot-nine and a hundred and fifty five pounds of Irish piss-and-vinegar, dropped his pick axe to mop his face.

"*Damn* it, Hannigan!" Derek "Hoss" Baumer yelled. It had taken Joe a while to place the face of his foreman, but after the first month or so, he remembered the red-faced man with the crew-cut who had taken such pleasure in lashing into the two men who had fought on their way to the complex, "Get yer' shit together! Ore ain't gonna' mine itself!"

"Sorry, sir," Hannigan removed the towel from his face, "It's just so damned *hot* down here—"

"I hear Detroit has a lot better weather this time'a year."

The mere mention of Joe's childhood hometown sent a chill down his spine. Had it only been a couple of decades ago that the Motor City was beginning to enjoy a renaissance? Bootstrapped up by tech companies and philanthropists eager to demonstrate that even the worst urban decay could be reversed, polished, and greened until it absolutely shined.

How long had the best of intentions taken to utterly devolve after The Announcement? A month? Two? It just went to show how quickly a city that had worked so hard to beat back the gangs, beat back the dredges of society could be overgrown with ills once more.

Not that it mattered. Let the gangbangers have their playground. At least the rest of the country hadn't lost its mind.

Yet.

The boogeyman of Detroit constantly loomed over Joe's shoulder. Every time he heard the word, he wasn't reminded of his awful past spent hustling on the streets at the behest of his junky mother.

Rather it was the specter of the grim future he faced there, without so much as a warning to Mason, that kept him swinging that pick axe, carving up pockets of ore, and generally keeping his mouth shut and head down.

Of course, Hoss didn't have to worry about Detroit at all. As long as his outfit met its quotas, he already had his ticket punched. All the more reason to lean on these men harder, and ensure that they created the precious ingot for the machines to forge into humanity's crowning achievement.

"No, sir. I'm minin', I'm minin'…" Hannigan did his best to conceal his disdain for the overbearing foreman.

Joe actually didn't begrudge Hoss coming down in the hole with his constantly-sunburned face and shiny crew cut to berate his charges. After all, Hoss had a job to do, too, even if the stakes were different. All of the workers desperately sought something they didn't have. Hoss already had what they wanted, but could lose it at any moment.

"Laaaa-DIES and Gentle-MENNN, it's three hours from quittin' time on day seven of week fifty-two. You're all close to meetin' yer' benchmarks so far, but we *will not* tolerate a slowdown. Just 'cause yer' counterparts in smelting are takin' it easy today doesn't mean that you get to do the same. Am I clear?"

"Sir, yes, sir!" everyone replied in unison.

"Terrrrr-iffic!" he accentuated the "r" and separated the syllables. "Happy mining, folks!"

Hoss marched up the hole, back stiff as a board.

"Ass," Hannigan said under his breath.

"'Can say that again," Joe shook his head.

On the other side of Joe, Wyatt chuckled as he paused to mop clumps of mud from his brow.

"Ass."

This caused Joe to choke out another laugh.

"You've been awful quiet today, Wyatt."

Wyatt grinned, "Had a dream last night I've been thinkin' about."

"Oh?" Joe raised an eyebrow, genuinely interested.

"Yeah, still workin' through it. I'll tell ya' more about it when I think through it more. Heavy stuff."

"Can't be heavier than what we're dealin' with here," Joe said.

"You'd be surprised," Wyatt answered. He shook his head as he stared through the rock before he turned to Joe, never ceasing to swing the pick axe as he continued to talk, "You must have some pleasant dreams, Joe."

Joe arched an eyebrow, "How do you figure?"

Ca-CHINK

Wyatt half-smiled through gritted teeth, "October 9, 2049."

"What about it?" Joe asked.

Ca-CHINK

"Taking on Washington?" Wyatt looked at Joe, "The four sack game?"

"Four-and-a-half, technically," Joe snorted.

"Regardless, you broke Timmy Ryan's school record. Shattered the damned thing, actually. And as a middle linebacker, no less! You were a monster, Joe."

Ca-CHINK

Joe shook his head, "That poor guard'a theirs, Andrews or somethin' like that, he had no idea what hit him."

Wyatt's eyes gleamed as Joe proceeded to detail every play of the game, every down, every nuance for the insatiable Southern Cal fan who worked alongside him.

As Joe finished his play-by-play recounting of the game, he heard a laugh from the opposite side of the tunnel.

"All'a that work, all'a that effort, and look where it got you now. Same place as us," Hannigan said.

Joe shrugged, "Guess you have a point, Danny."

Ca-CHINK

His attention turned back to the rock marred by increasingly deep, narrow tracks as the pick axe cleaved through the wall. Without the pleasant distraction of Wyatt's endless curiosity, Joe's arms went heavy and slack. He slowed his pick axe down enough and reflexively checked his watch, though his eyes gravitated not toward the time, but rather the date:

"July 18th"

Had it been a year already? he thought.

A year spent in the middle-of-nowhere Nevada.

A year since everything had changed.

He shook off the thought.

Better off now, anyway. Joe thought. *At least a man knows where he stands here.*

The miners worked into the darkness, their work illuminated by the intense halogen bulbs that littered the site. Every eighth cartload, it was Joe's turn to push the alloy up the tracks to the top of the mine, where the smelting crew would take it and roll it the rest of the way to the smelters, which belched thick, black smoke into the otherwise pristine sky nearly twenty-four hours a day.

Use it or lose it, Joe thought.

Titanium hauling duty was considered some of the easier mining work available, since the ore tended to be lighter than some of the other materials the miners pulled from the Earth. The worst was uranium duty; Joe could've sworn the pale, yellow powder seeped in through the seams of his flimsy suit and was responsible for the harsh cough he had developed.

What am I going to do? File a worker's comp claim? Joe smiled at his own suggestion as he handed the cart off to two of his nameless counterparts, who accepted the ore with little more than a nod.

The whistle blew and Joe slouched as he finally allowed his aching muscles to go slack. The abject agony from his first days on mining duty had dulled to a throbbing, constant pain that pulled at his muscles, and dragged his usually imposing frame into a crouch.

The worst is almost over, he reminded himself.

Or was it? Though mining was incredibly difficult, the specter of two more years of other kinds of painstaking labor still loomed in front of him.

And yet, that wasn't the worst part. No, the kicker of it all was that he'd sacrifice so much of his body, of his mind, of his humanity in subjecting himself to this awful nightmare, and in the end, none of it would likely matter.

FOUR

Joe hauled himself through the complex. He arrived at a clear glass partition and placed his hand on the pad next to the sliding door.

It took the machine a fraction of a second to recognize the former linebacker's handprint and turn green.

"Welcome home, Mr. Grissom," a soothing, female voice said.

"Uh…hi there," Joe said. Even if the computer didn't care, he still felt odd not saying anything in reply.

He turned right down the hallway and counted the doors to his left:

One.

Two.

Three.

At the fourth door, he stopped and fumbled for the keys on his belt. He mumbled something unintelligible as he shook out the key to the door and stuck it in the lock.

The door swung open. It was all Joe could do to stagger over to the gently-worn (if thoroughly modern) faux-leather sofa and heave his large frame into it.

"Hey Dad," Mason was already hard at work, cooking dinner in the kitchenette on the far side of the room.

"Hay is for horses," Joe covered his eyes with his forearm. He blinked his heavy lids several times and rubbed his hands on his face before he forced himself to sit up on the couch with a hearty sigh. "How was school?"

"Eh, better. I'm doin' better in science and math."

Joe forced himself not to grin, "Good. That's real good. You keep that up now."

"I know, I know. Every 'A' helps."

Joe nodded, "Damn straight it does." he wobbled to his feet and labored over to his kitchen, hiding his pain with a well-practiced grimace disguised as a grin.

"What you makin' tonight?" Joe asked.

"Spaghetti. It's been over a year, Dad."

Joe's mind raced back to the night when everything had changed, when for the first time, in the span of thirty commercial-free minutes of television, he came to understand just what was important in his life, what exactly held *meaning*.

Though it didn't ease the sting that the fragrant smells of the marinara sauce shot deep into his heart, he nonetheless made a point of taking in two deep sniffs of the stuff and forcing a thin smile.

"Smells delicious. We may need to update your profile."

"Aw, come on, Dad."

"No, no, I'm serious. Every 'A' helps, every skill helps, too. There're worse things than bein' a chef, ya' know."

Joe winced as his knee wobbled. He leaned on the kitchen chair before he awkwardly slid it out and cast his body into it.

"After dinner, we're gonna' drill again, see if you can't pass the public safety exam. They say that gives you five more entries."

Mason coughed and nodded. The change in the boy since they had arrived jarred Joe. Not but a year ago, he was sure Mason would've come up with some cockamamie excuse to play hologames or watch movies—*anything* but study for "some boring test."

Now, his son was focused. Driven. Much like the miners, each day, each *moment*, had become life-and-death, with far too much time dedicated to dreading the latter rather than appreciating the former.

Yet they *had* to. Especially when there were only a finite number of tomorrows.

Joe clicked the holodisplay on and saw the SSCTV logo floating behind the attractive, vaguely Asian female news anchor.

"…the cat's name is Roderick, and he's been providing much needed morale for Delta Wing," she shifted in her seat, though her delivery remained overly sunny, "On a more serious note, the U.S. missile defense shield intercepted yet another ICBM headed for Starship City in the Nevada desert. The launch was apparently a joint Russian-Chinese attempt to cripple America's self-described 'Hail Mary' effort, but a combination of jet-mounted lasers and—"

Joe hit several buttons on the remote and *Back to the Future* came up. It was a classic, one that Joe had watched countless times. He didn't like the remake nearly as much; there was something comforting about a simpler time, when people knew little and worried less, that appealed to him.

"Tell you what, son—why don't we throw the ball around a bit after dinner before we get to work on your public safety studyin'. Sound good?"

This time Mason struggled to hide his grin, "Yeah. Sure, sounds fine."

"'Cause if you'd rather jump right into studyin' that's not a problem."

"No, no, throwin' the ball for a bit sounds great, Dad."

They hastily gobbled down the spaghetti. Marty McFly and Doc Brown diverted Joe's attention from the various forms of hatred directed at *that woman* that boiled to the surface.

Joe's muscles screamed for relief, maybe a warm bath or massage, but he knew he'd never see either again, not for the rest of his short life.

As he grabbed the game ball from the 2049 Rose Bowl (though Mason had no way of knowing or appreciating its importance), Joe realized that before The Announcement, he could count the number of times he had a catch with Mason on one hand. He had always been too tired, too worried, too occupied.

And with what? "Life?" He snorted at the thought. Maybe this wasn't so bad after all. Even if he was forced to cram a lifetime of memories into three short years, maybe the quality of those years far surpassed all of the "will"s and "someday"s that would soon turn into "wished"s and "should've"s.

They made their way outside and Joe couldn't help but admire the night sky, inky blue, but with millions of pinpricks of light that forced their way to the fore.

Which one will they choose? he thought. For a brief moment, he wished he had paid more attention in his astronomy class at Southern Cal.

Then he remembered that he only took astronomy because his first choice, GEO 105, widely known as "rocks for jocks" at the sport-centric school, was full, and Joe had overslept on the day course registration lists were to be submitted online.

Yet as his eyes drifted skyward, they were drawn to a small, bright red dot that was only slightly larger than the others that pocked the night sky. His pupils dilated as the light from the orb didn't twinkle so much as it pulsed, in synch with Joe's own heartbeat.

Womp...womp...womp...

As Joe lifted the football above his shoulder, a verse popped into his head, deep from within his subconscious.

The words terrified him even as he released the ball and it sailed toward Mason, who handled it deftly.

"Don't catch with your body!" Joe said. "Use your hands!"

Even as he chided his son, who nodded obediently, the phrase ran through his mind over and over again, a mantra sparing him no relief:

This is the harbinger of your destruction.

The world started to spin. Joe looked at Mason for reassurance, but his innocent, playful glance only worsened Joe's paranoia that most likely neither of them would be alive a few short years from now, not because of anything they did or did not do, but rather due to complete chance, the utter randomness of a universe that did, indeed, play dice.

As he surveyed the desert skyline, though, his eye caught a glimpse of something glistening in the pale moonlight. It was their only hope, their salvation amidst so much pain and sorrow.

The gigantic starship was still a frame, constantly added onto by the 3D printers and the assembly crew, which would rotate into the mines shortly.

Poor bastards, Joe thought, if only for a moment.

His breathing calmed as humanity's last great hope, its refuge from the approaching red menace, stood defiantly, evading even Chinese-Russian annihilation by nuclear-freaking-weapons.

He knew he'd never set foot upon the *Minerva*, he'd never live out the childhood fantasy, however fleeting, of becoming an astronaut.

But as he hauled in Mason's pass, looking past the tight spiral of the ball to the boy's laughing, innocent eyes, Joe made a promise to himself.

That ship is our salvation, he thought.

And I'll do anything to make sure my boy gets on it.

FIVE

As Joe pushed yet another cartload of uranium ore toward the processing bot in smelter 41A, he couldn't help but choke out a few words.

"This stuff *stinks*."

Not the uranium itself; uranium was paradoxically odorless and tasteless, a silent assassin waiting to slay those who didn't respect its lethal power.

Rather he was referring to smelting duty, which had somehow proved to be even worse than toiling in the mines. At least in the mines he saw the fruits of his labor, could feel the pick axe cut and dig through the ore deposits, and, most importantly, could usually wear relatively comfortable, loose-fitting clothing or coveralls.

In the smelter, though, all he felt was the never-ending heat of the blast furnace, amplified by the thin, yet suffocating, Tyvek suits they had to wear constantly, as they loaded and unloaded cartfuls of ore to be processed

34

into ingot that the 3-D printers could use, both pre-and-post-launch.

Helluva time for them to be concerned about our health, Joe thought.

His body poured off sweat in buckets, his vision blurred by wayward streams of perspiration. He raised a forearm to clear his face, but the respirator blocked his way.

He snorted. *It's my last shift,* Joe thought. The heat was unbearable, and despite the radiation risk, in the face of a far greater and more lethal power, Joe peeled off the usual flimsy, paper-and-polymer protective suit in favor of the freedom and comfort of his undershirt and broken-in jeans.

He gulped in deep lungfuls of cool air as he shook off the perspiration like a wet, angry dog. He pushed the cart down the track like a blocking sled.

Wyatt raised an eyebrow. He did his best to keep up; usually he could only manage to wrap his spindly hands around the left side of the cart and chop his legs as quickly as possible to match his powerful counterpart.

About halfway down the track, Joe stopped and grabbed the small of his back. It screamed like metal being cold-twisted as he fell first to his knees, then onto the track.

"Joe? Joe!" Wyatt yelled. "Get up! You don't want—"

"What don't he want, Wyatt?" Hoss Baumer's booming southern voice resonated around the steel walls like a mallet striking a gong. "He don't want to wear his damned suit?"

Wyatt offered his hand to the fallen man, "Get up," he hissed.

Joe's head raced. *One day away...one day away...* he thought. He wriggled on the floor for several moments before, out of sheer exhaustion, memories began to flash through his head. There he was with Madison, on their wedding day. There she was, calmly starting the car and driving away, away from her bawling son and stoic husband, without so much as a second glance.

As the scene unfolded in his mind, his thoughts turned to Mason, the lanky kid who had held his hand on that trek through the desert those two years ago, who had worked so hard to pass his public safety test, and for what? So that he had five more meaningless entries in the lottery to end all lotteries? For spots on the ship promised to millions but limited to tens of thousands?

Nonetheless, Joe gritted his teeth as he rose to one knee, then ignored the searing pain in the joint to rise to his full height. Without thinking, he bent his legs through the excruciating pain once more and started to push the cart unprompted.

"Eh, eh, eh..." Hoss boomed. He wagged a meaty finger at the fallen ex-linebacker. "I don't give half a yella' *damn* if you don't care about makin' the ship, Grissom. I don't care if you're plannin' on makin' it, or you have a family member who passed through or whatever. Not wearin' your suit while handling uranium ore is about the most reckless thing you can do in this here city—" he reached for his belt and produced a stinger stick, its two prongs, already screaming with electricity, "—and I don't take kindly to my workers bein' reckless."

Joe opened his mouth to speak, but instead found himself gasping for air as Hoss swung the stick down at him. Joe's eyes rolled back in his head. His enormous body seized before it began spasming uncontrollably. The pain welled in his chest; his heart thundered like it was going to burst as his eyes bulged in their sockets.

The prongs had only touched him for a second, but they left a stinging mark on his stomach, already throbbing as a result of the two years of constant manual labor he had performed.

Even as the tears poured from Joe's eyes, he heard Wyatt's sharp protests.

"Aw, come on, Hoss, was that really necessary?"

"Yep. But this isn't."

The foreman lowered the stick and its sizzling prongs on the blonde-haired worker still in his suit. Wyatt tried to speak as the tool hit its mark, which left him babbling an incoherent string of repetitive, guttural cries as he doubled over, then fell flat on his face.

Joe tried to push himself up, but every couple of seconds his arm would go weak and he'd crash to the floor once more. He must've been covered in uranium dust by now, but that was the least of his concerns as he struggled to regain anything more than momentary control over his body.

"Maybe that'll teach ya' to wear your suit next time," Hoss spat the words at Joe before he turned to Wyatt, "And *you* to keep yer' damned *dumb* smart mouth shut."

Hoss left to antagonize the next crew as the two men lay on the ground, writhing in pain for several minutes before the spasms finally ceased enough for Joe to get his bearings and force himself to one knee.

"Was it worth it?" Wyatt asked.

Joe shot him an ugly look.

"That's what I thought."

"I'm sick of this crap, Wyatt. Why do we have to give up our damned freedom, our damned *humanity*, just for the slimmest of chances to be picked to go on a *starship*, that has about as much chance'a makin' it where it's goin' as I do of bein' *alive* three years from now."

Wyatt grinned as his muscles calmed enough for him to stagger to his feet.

"You know that dream I told ya' about?"

Joe raised an eyebrow, "Dream?"

"Yeah, 'bout a year ago. Actually, exactly a year ago—last day in the mines. Hoss was threatenin' to send Hannigan to Detroit."

Joe furrowed his brow as he thought back to that day. Had it been a year already? Another year of backbreaking work? A year of Mason cooking dinner for the two of them? A year of playing catch in the front yard of the complex, each night looking up, hoping that the red menace in the sky would get smaller, disappointed when it did the opposite?

Wyatt stuck a hand out, "Doesn't matter. I've been thinkin' 'bout that dream for damn near a year now. Reason I didn't tell anyone is that it was about, you know, the lottery.

"It was selection day. That damned spaceship was bigger than any skyscraper I ever *seen*. All gleamin' and brushed, with an American flag painted on the side—it was beautiful. Ridiculous, but absolutely beautiful.

"You were there. So was your kid. And Hannigan. And we waited. And waited. And waited. And it came down to the last name to be called, and I remember, the President, she was standin' up at the front and she hit the button for the last name, and it came up:

"'Wyatt Port,' she said. I had a grin like a sixteen year-old in a whorehouse. The greyshirts descended on me and dragged me up to the front. Got to ride in the monorail with the President herself, very posh, the whole nine.

"But then, when we got to the ship, they let the President and the greyshirts on, but threw me off to the side. There was a guy in a dark suit and sunglasses there, and he had the sickest smile I've ever seen on his face, the kind'a smile that would give a kid nightmares for a month.

"Well this guy turns to me as I'm about to get on and sticks out his hand. 'Sorry fella,' he says. 'All full.'

"And so I say, 'Wait just a minute! I was picked. I *won* the lottery!'

"And he looks at me with this weird grimace, like he swallowed an army'a ants, and the grin that churned my stomach pops up again, and he says, 'Didn't you know? The list was picked ahead of time.'

"He leans in real close to me, and the words practically slither out of his mouth, 'All of this has…meant…*nothing!*'"

Wyatt's eyes went wide, though Joe compensated by narrowing his own.

"So?"

"Whattaya *mean* 'so'? Don't ya' get it? Don't ya' ever worry that we're bein' *had*? That there *are* no extra spots on the ship? That we're doin' all'a this for the government, or I don't know, maybe something *bigger* than the government, and we'll just be left millin' around when the fireworks show starts?"

Joe lowered a skeptical eye at his friend, "You think I don't worry about that *every day*? Put yourself in my shoes, Wyatt—imagine that you have all'a those same thoughts, all'a the crazy dreams and everything, all of the nagging doubts that add up, gnaw at your mind.

"Then imagine that you have a kid, a son who you'd do anything for. You would—you *did*—sell yourself into damned *slavery* voluntarily for him, all for the longest of shots, the slimmest of chances that his smile, his eyes, his laugh, *all* of the things that make him the most important thing in my world will get to grow up, live, and be *damned* with a family of his own some day."

Wyatt snorted a laugh.

Joe scowled.

Wyatt composed himself, "Look, all I'm sayin' is that," he looked around to make sure that Hoss or one of the other forepeople were around before he leaned in and whispered, "I've been askin' around, trollin' some of the seedier corners of this place. I hear there are ways, less public ways, to get what you want. Might involve gettin' your hands a little dirty—"

"And a one-way trip to Detroit for both me and my son?" Joe asked.

Wyatt ignored him, "—but a guy like you, with your size, is in high demand with those sorts of folks. High demand."

"Thanks for the tip," Joe said, either unwilling or unable to mop up the dripping sarcasm.

"Don't mention it," Wyatt responded in kind. He looked at his friend, caked head-to-toe in Uranium dust, "You, uh, might wanna' get a shower or somethin'. You know, 'fore you pick up something pesky like radiation poisoning."

Even though Joe nodded and forced a smile, he was jarred by Wyatt's explanation of his dream, and all of the potential implications. Should he trust a government that would condone whatever this project had become? What if they *were* all being had? What if there *was* no room on the ship, no chance for his son?

Worse still, the thoughts running through his mind weren't of the "they can't!" or "they wouldn't!" variety, but rather one simple summation of everything he had been through in the Nevada desert to date:

We'll see...

SIX

Compared to Joe's first two work shifts, finishing and quality control was a walk in the park.

Not that Joe found conversing with robots and wrenching redundant rivets into place ("Just in case those put in by the machines failed," Hoss Baumer had boomed on the first day) particularly fascinating or rewarding.

But compared to chipping out ores or hauling them around smelters, Joe found the relative boredom to be a relief.

He lay on his back down a corridor called "G-7" somewhere in *Minerva's* enormous habitation ring, and fastened another backup bolt into place underneath a vanity.

Not sure why these *are so damned important,* Joe thought.

Then it dawned on him:

They were almost done.

Three years, gone, in the blink of the eye.

I thought time was only supposed to fly if you were having fun, Joe thought. Ironically, the wrench slipped the thread and fell out of Joe's hand, tumbling until it hit the floor with a loud "CLANG!"

As he muttered a muffled curse word, he heard a round of slow, deliberate applause from the entrance. His eyes drifted upward to find the upside-down form of Wyatt in the doorway.

"You're late," Joe deadpanned.

Wyatt mopped his soaked brow, even as he softened his friend's statement with a wry grin.

"Sorry boss," he shrugged, "was a bit under the weather."

"Oh?" Joe raised an eyebrow.

Wyatt waved off his concern, "Yeah, they say it's nothin' too big, just a virus. Meds should calm the symptoms down in a coupl'a days. Should still be outta' my system in a few weeks, well before the big lottery, no problem."

Joe exhaled a half-sigh of relief. He turned over and crawled out of the space under the vanity.

"Well that's good. Glad to hear it."

"You and me both," Wyatt said. "'Miss anything exciting?"

"Other than my damn clumsy hands?" Joe asked. He shook out his right hand for effect.

"Hell, I remember when those hands hauled down Heisman winner Rusty Tennison of *the* Ohio State University with ten seconds left to win the Rose Bowl."

"It was eleven seconds," Joe allowed the hint of a smile to creep over the corner of his mouth.

"It was zero seconds before they could get lined up again and run another play."

Joe smiled. If he was honest with himself, Wyatt's overindulgent accounts of his collegiate exploits were part of the reason the two had become so close over these past three years, despite the ample contempt that their proximity should have bred if one believes the old axiom.

"Didn't you get the game ball from that one?" Wyatt asked.

Joe nodded.

"What happened to it?"

Joe thought about lying for a moment, then realized how ridiculous it would be to do so.

"I throw it around with Mason, every night. Even when it rains."

Joe may as well have told Wyatt he was using the Shroud of Turin as a bath towel.

"Are you *kidding?!* That thing should be…"

"Should be *what?*" Joe asked.

"Should be in, like, a *museum* or somethin'."

Joe shook his head, "It's a relic from a football game that most folks've forgotten. Nothin' more, nothin' less."

"It was the formative experience of my—"

Joe and Wyatt had had this conversation numerous times before. This time, though, Joe decided to pull out his trump card. He reached in his pocket and pulled out a small, gold trinket. He held the thick, pyramid-shaped ruby out toward the still-sweating U.S.C. fan.

"My God…is that—?"

"The ring," Joe said. "Go ahead, put it on if you like."

"Are you *serious*?" Wyatt asked.

"Hell, Wyatt, it's prob'ly just gonna' be blasted to dust in a couple years' time like everything else, anyway. Put it on."

Wyatt didn't waste any time. He slid the enormous ring on one of his spindly fingers. It circled the bony digit like a kid trying on his father's wedding ring.

"There was a time when I thought that thing would never leave my finger," Joe said.

"What happened?" Wyatt asked.

Joe shrugged, "Don't rightly know. Probably the whole pro thing."

Newly emboldened by the monstrous piece of jewelry on his finger, Wyatt took a deep breath. He leveled his gaze at Joe's large, tired, dark eyes.

"Did you fix the game, Joe?"

Joe rolled his eyes, "Really? I make it through almost three *years* without this shit, and now—"

Wyatt waved away the question, "Forget it. Sorry. It was wrong of me to bring it up."

Joe stroked his chin for several moments as the awkward silence choked the room.

"Yes."

"Yes *what?*" Wyatt asked.

"Yes, I fixed the game."

Wyatt took one cautious step forward, then another. His tremulous ear leaned in as he thought about how best to approach this very delicate situation.

"You *fixed* an *NFL* game?" Wyatt asked.

Joe nodded, "Haven't told anyone up 'til now. Even the ex-wife, though she's wily enough she prob'ly figured it out somewhere along the way."

"But why? You were gonna' be a star, sure as hell!"

Joe steeled his jaw as he turned to face the desert landscape through the tiny window in the quarters.

"Madison just had Mason about a year or two before. We weren't married yet or nothin', and my stupid agent ran off with my signing bonus. I was desperate for cash—I had a family to feed. So this guy, real shady Italian-lookin' fella', he corners me out at a bar one night. Asks me if I've ever heard the name 'Meyer Smitts.' I say, no, I haven't. Turns out he's some big-time gangster."

"Meyer *Smitts?*" Wyatt asked. He swallowed.

"Yeah. So this guy says, 'wanna make a quick ten mil? And I say 'yeah.' And he says, 'make sure you guys lose on Sunday—and lose *big*."

"But, how—" Wyatt's fandom got the better of him, "—*how* can you do that as a linebacker?"

"*Middle* linebacker, Wyatt. I made all'a the calls in the huddle. Played it straight the first half, then started messin' up calls, puttin' guys in the wrong positions on key downs. Before you knew it, Dallas was up by twenty-one, and I was gettin' my ass chewed out by coach. 'Grissom, you dumb S.O.B.! I've *never* seen someone so *stupid* in my twenty years of coaching football!'"

Joe shrugged again, "After that, I got benched, then the press heard a rumor about 'game-fixin'" and the team had to release me." Joe snorted, "Worst part was, I blew all that cash in some damned-*fool* real estate deal. Within' five years'a bein' out of the league, I was swingin' a hammer, workin' construction," he cast his eyes downward, "a damned *failure*."

Joe took a deep breath, "And every day since that Sunday, I've vowed that if I ever have to trade my integrity for money, or anything else I wanted in the heat of the moment, I'd remember how I felt at the end of that game, sick to my stomach, unable to look my teammates in the eye, guys who had sweated and *bled* for me, and never do something so damned *stupid* again."

He stuck out his hand. It took Wyatt a minute to process the gesture, but he sheepishly produced the ring. Joe slid it back into his pocket.

"I'm guessin' you'll also be the *last* person I ever tell that to."

Wyatt nodded. He was desperate to change the subject, "You think after *Minerva* takes off they'll still play sports, Joe?"

Joe's eyes bulged for a moment before he composed himself, "Sure...sure they will, Wyatt."

Satisfied, his friend smiled.

Joe looked at the wrench, which lay carelessly on the floor. He could've sworn he heard Hoss's footsteps clanging down the curved hallway outside of the door.

"Lemme' help you with that," Wyatt made a motion for the wrench.

Joe stuck out his hand, "I got it, Wyatt. I got it."

He picked up the tool and the two men began wrenching away, side-by-side once more.

SEVEN

June 29th, 2066
T-Minus 21 days, 13 hours, 41 minutes

Joe rubbed his temples. Over the past few days, the dull ache baked into his bones had migrated up to his head, where it settled and thundered away at his mind like a symphony of jackhammers.

He entered his apartment to find Mason slumped on the couch, beads of sweat dripping down his face. Joe wasn't shocked to see the Starship City news on the holovision; an edict had come down from the Powers That Be at t-minus thirty days that the news would automatically be broadcast from every television in the complex each evening.

In his former life, such a pronouncement would've infuriated Joe.

At that moment, though, he merely shrugged it off: he'd endured far worse.

The Asian anchorwoman who had been so sunny years before now perfected her grave expression.

"As you can see, the first images of Destiny en route to Earth have been captured by the Gleiser deep-space telescope—"

A snarling, nasty red planet surrounded by thick clouds shot out of the screen toward the viewer.

"—revealing the stark truth and gravity of humanity's—and indeed all of the Earth's—dire situation. Leading scientists have confirmed that the rogue planet is directly on course to hit the Earth a little over two years from today."

Inexplicably, her face lit up with a smile, "But as brave, courageous, willing participants in the U.S.'s Starship City program, you're still on track to have a shot at a seat on *Minerva*, the spaceship that's set to be completed twenty days from now and summarily launched to the stars. The members of the List thank you for your tireless dedication and hard work over these past two years and eleven-plus months, but remember, there's still plenty to do over the next three weeks to test the ship and ensure its timely completion."

"Wish you could turn that garbage off," Joe said.

Mason forced a thin smile, "I tried. They set it up so you can't."

Joe nodded, "I know." He looked at his son and wrinkled his brow, "You turn the A.C. off?"

Mason eyes sank in their sockets, his usually lively, handsome countenance dripping with sweat as he wheezed out breath-after-breath.

Joe's eyes went wide. He shook his head, "No...it's not...it's probably just—"

"Just *what*, Dad? Allergies? In the damned *desert*?"

"No...no it *can't* be. You *can't* be sick. Not now. Not when you're so close, *so*—" he hit an empty spot on the sofa, "—damned *close*."

The sixteen year old was too tired to do anything but sigh.

"It's...it's okay, Dad. We knew it was gonna' be long odds when we signed up. They just won't let someone sick as me on the—"

Joe shook his head as he slammed the couch once more, "No. No, not like *this*, damn it! All the hours, the *years*. Son, I—"

Mason's lip quivered. Though his face had already taken on the lean lines of adulthood, any hint of that façade was shattered as his eyes glistened and his breaths became heaving sobs.

"I'm sorry, dad. It's my fault," Mason brought a sleeve up to his face.

Joe's snarl dropped. He put a thick arm around his son and drew him in tight, until Mason sobbed into his shoulder. He cradled the young man's head in his massive palm as he shook his head.

As he did so, he heard a voice inside of his head. Not his own familiar inner monologue, but rather Wyatt's pleasant lilt.

Yeah, they say it's nothin' too big, just a virus. Meds should calm the symptoms down in a coupl'a days. Should still make the big lottery, no problem.

To underscore the point, another wave of pain swept through Joe's head, followed by the twinge of nausea that had haunted him the past several days.

And he remembered:

The ring.

Joe gritted his teeth. His chest rose and fell with each pained lungful of air. How could he be so careless?! *So* close to the end of this insanity? What he thought was a little harmless catharsis for a beaten-down friend would end up costing his son his slimmest of chances to make it off this giant rock before another one happened to hurtle through the same tiny speck of the infinite vastness of space?

Even as the thought struggled to form inside of his pounding mind, he knew it was a lie.

It wasn't Wyatt who he was trying to cheer up. It wasn't Wyatt who needed to regain his piece of mind, especially about something as meaningless as football.

It was himself.

Joe wanted to run out into the desert, far away from this phony apartment in a city built virtually overnight to accommodate the hordes that worked the land, pillaged it, damned near *raped* it for those precious few who would eventually cart the precious resources somewhere else, far away, and do with it what they would. He yearned to be away from that damned spaceship and its List, and the lucky other few to get on board.

Instead, he choked back the emotions through gritted teeth. Blood rushed to his face and seemed to boil off his skin as sweat. He gripped his son tightly, his brain still struggling to come up with a plan.

There's always a plan.

His face dropped once more as he realized the dire straights they now faced.

Until there's not.

"I'm sorry, Dad."

Joe pulled away from his son and put his hands on the young man's shoulders. He gazed into those eyes, those formerly starry, bright orbs that were now red and soaked with terror. Joe fought through the anger and the pain, through all of the churning mass that his insides had become to focus on those eyes, now burnt out after years of hope, no matter how foolish and misplaced it had been.

Hope.

"No, *I'm* sorry, son," Joe said. "I…someone else at work was sick, and like a damned fool, I didn't get it checked out. You got it from me."

"Dad, I—"

Joe shook his head and leveled his gaze, "You listen to *me*, son," he patted his chest, "It's on me. It's my fault. *I'm* sorry. If there's anything I could do to fix it, *anything* in the *world*, I—"

Before he could even form the rest of the thought, his eyes went wide. A thunderclap of agony shot through his head, and in its aftermath, the solution presented itself.

As the dark realization came to him, Joe didn't so much as flinch.

"I have an idea."

EIGHT

Joe unfolded the small piece of paper. The tiny sheet had been forced into his hand by an attractive brunette who passed by the hallway right outside of his door earlier that evening.

On it was a convoluted list of instructions and an address, the same one that adorned the nameplate next to the door he found himself in front of.

"314 Scarab Lane," it read in highly stylized script.

Joe had never heard of a "Scarab Lane," and certainly hadn't been within a mile of this part of Starship City. Yet here, amidst the storage lockers containing various spare parts for assembly bots, appeared to be a proper residence, albeit one without many friendly neighbors.

He knocked three times in rapid succession, followed by two longer, heavier knocks, as the paper instructed.

After several seconds, the door opened to a locker very similar to the rest. As far as Joe could tell, the only difference between this locker and the others was the man in front of him wearing a burnt orange leather vest over his bare torso and a cowboy hat, which framed his tan, stubbly face and long, dark hair. That he nearly matched Joe's size made the tiny toothpick that jutted out from the gap between his front two teeth all the more comical.

"Yeah?" the man in the cowboy hat asked. He puffed out his chest to attempt to fill Joe's frame.

"Luminos," Joe said, with a hint of an amused smile.

The man pulled his vest back to show Joe the awful, hissing, pronged metal stinger stick attached to his belt.

"Nothin' funny, Sunshine," he said with a grin.

Joe nodded. The cowboy waited until the door swung shut automatically before he turned and tapped several spots on the sparse concrete wall in rapid succession.

A green light shone, and Joe steeled his jaw as the seemingly-solid wall separated to reveal the last thing he expected.

It was a room, but not like the simple, comfortable apartment that Joe and Mason occupied. This place was at least five or six times the size of theirs, and adorned with all manner of fountains and greenery. The marble floor squeaked as rough-looking, leather-clad types chased after beautiful, bare-footed, togaed women (and a handful of equally attractive men) who giggled as they fluttered about the room.

Joe disguised a sniffle as he took in the fragrant aromas of fruits and flowers, smells that seemed foreign to his nostrils after so many days alternating between the horrid stenches of solvents and ingot in the mines and smelters, and the over-processed, sanitized air of *Minerva* and the rest of the facility.

Giant picture windows framed the view of *Minerva* at the front of the room, from an angle that Joe had never seen the ship before. While it usually stood ominous watch over the apartments, reminding their inhabitants of their only potential salvation, here it seemed distant and proud, defiantly waiting to carry those lucky thousands off of their doomed planet.

In front of the windows was a throne (*a* throne! Joe thought), and upon it sat a reclining, fortiesh man draped in purple robes with an olive wreath perched atop his curly black hair. Two more gorgeous women attended to him, one doting on him and laughing at nearly every word to leave his mouth while the other fanned him with a giant palm leaf and shot daggers at her counterpart.

The man in purple laughed as he brought a bejeweled chalice to his lips and greedily guzzled down its contents. He wiped away the dark violet remnants that dribbled down his chin as Joe and the cowboy approached.

"Anyway, the guy starts getting all uppity, 'that's not *my* truck!' So I say to him, 'Hey, whatta' I look like? The DMV?'"

The beautiful woman attending to the purple-robed man laughed until she nearly cried, even if the vacant look in her eye belied her comprehension of the story.

Joe raised an eyebrow as the man on the throne turned his attention toward the two large men making their way across the polished marble floor, resolute amid the tomfoolery.

The purple-robed man's expression brightened as he waved a flimsy, ring-adorned hand at the two men.

"Ah, here he is now! Joseph Grissom, as I live and breathe!"

Joe met the man's gaze. Though Joe was still working through the indolence of his surroundings, he recognized the man who had caused him such anguish, such despair through the years without so much as even a meeting.

"Mr. Smitts," he nodded.

"Please, call me Meyer!" Smitts shook his glass as he raised it. This time, the purple liquid spilled out onto the woman next to him.

She giggled in response and made coy eyes at the new arrival.

"Whatever you want, sir," Joe said.

Smitts's eyes went wide as he rose from his chair and put an arm around Joe, "Joseph, my good man, I assure you, despite the decadence on display, I am, at heart, a simple man. Meyer, May, any part of my first name will do. Besides, I owe quite a lot to you, my good man."

Joe raised an eyebrow.

Smitts leaned in and placed the back of his hand over his mouth.

"Thanks for your help back in 'fifty. Really," he formed the "okay" sign around the neck of his chalice, "set me up well."

The veins in Joe's neck bulged. He struggled against the urge to take the man by the neck and throw him around the room like a rag doll.

Instead he smiled and shrugged.

"'Nothin' of it."

Smitts jabbed Joe in the ribs, "This guy made me over a hundred mill in a day. Dare I say set up," he waved his arms in wide arcs around the room, cup and all, "all of this. Or, at least, helped me plant the seeds for the fantastic journey that awaits once that monstrosity," he waved at the window, "*finally* leaves this damned planet, and I *do* mean that in the truest sense of the word."

Joe raised an eyebrow, "This is, uh, quite a place," he managed.

Meyer beamed as he paced in front of Joe, "You like it!? Yes, I'm sure it's not quite what you were accustomed to back in the day, eh, Joseph? But I think it'll serve us well going forward, plenty of clearance, well beyond the radius, for the important work we have to do once that ship is gone."

"Speaking of *Minerva*—"

Smitts cut him off, "I'm sure you're *dying* to know 'why?' Why bother with all of this if this planet is to be ground to dust in just two short years?"

"Actually, I—"

"I believe it was Rousseau who said that 'Every man has a right to risk his own life for the preservation of it.' A pithy quotation, but one that fits our current circumstances, nonetheless. Wouldn't you agree?"

Joe nodded.

"Of course, Rousseau also believed in the sanctity of a 'social contract.' That we give up our liberty in exchange for the benefits of living in civil society."

Smitts paused and turned to look at Joe over his shoulder, "Looks like the government's about to give up their end of the bargain."

He turned to face the giant window, "A lucky handful—albeit thousands, but in the grand scheme of things, a tiny few—jetting off to the stars as humanity's last gasp, their last hope to survive, and maybe even thrive, elsewhere in the galaxy, around some distant star that *might* have a habitable planet circling it.

"All important government officials, all sense of the rule of law—" Smitts clapped, "gone, in an instant." He pointed at the ship in the distance, "Once *that* leaves, you know what's left?" His lip curled into a smarmy grin, "It's the wild west, my friend. Lawlessness, every man for himself, mass chaos, hysteria, the works!"

The woman formerly at Smitts's side still giggled.

"Sounds great," Joe deadpanned.

Smitts lifted a finger, "Ah, but it is, my dear old friend. You see, when I first heard of this operation, this cockamamie plan to create a lottery to the stars, who do you think recognized this very problem? Who saw the droves of displaced refugees, huddling together, not caring whether they die now or two years from now, when Destiny finally slams into this pathetic little rock and grinds it to *dust*?"

Meyer thumbed his chest, "Me. Yours truly. If there's one thing I've learned in all of my years on this," he caught himself for a moment to smile grimly and chuckle, "planet, it's that people respond to one thing: hope. Hell, it's why you're here, right?" He looked at Joe for approval.

Joe stared back.

Meyer grinned, "Hope that something can ease their pain, their suffering, that someone will suddenly announce, 'just kidding! All a big joke!'" Smitts laughed.

Joe snorted.

"Which is why they'll look to a symbol, a beacon somewhere in the wilderness to congregate, a place that'll be kept safe, outside of the mobs and rape gangs, a place where people can not only live their lives, but celebrate the end of the world!"

"Starship City," Joe nodded.

"Yes! Exactly right my good friend! Starship City. The bastion of lawfulness in a world absent of it. Where," he motioned around the room, "the classical Greek and Roman ideals still will hold currency. Where people can have one last chance to live their final two years how *they* want to, while preserving the very social contract that Rousseau harped on his entire life!"

Joe raised a skeptical eyebrow.

I'm sure all of the morons in togas will love *it*, he thought.

Smitts turned back to face Joe, "Of course, this place won't run itself. We'll need peacekeepers. I'll need men, *and* women," he turned to acknowledge the tittering girl who still sat on the throne before he nodded at a couple of rougher, leather-clad women, one of whom led a togaed simpleton of a man around on a leash, "to help keep this thing together. I'll need an inner circle to dispatch justice *and* injustice as we see fit—as the place demands."

A cheshire grin washed over Smitts's face, "Which brings me to you, Joseph.

"I've been apprised of your vexing problem. Terrible business, sick kid and whatnot. Especially since, according to my good doctor," he nodded at a dyed-red, middle-aged woman being attended to by two adonis-like men in togas, anachronistic tattoos be damned, "Your boy poses no threat to the ship or its crew.

"I'm a team player, Joseph. I'm a patriot, first and foremost. Far be it from me to wish sickness on 'humanity's last hope.' But I needed to know that your boy won't cause the mission to fail, and thusly, I apologize for the delay in responding to your query."

"Nothin' of it," Joe shook his head.

"Now that I know that he's, for all intents and purposes, clean, I'm willing to make you a very generous offer, Joseph. One that I believe to be more than fair given the circumstances."

"Look, Mister—Meyer," Joe widened his eyes, "All I want is for my boy to have a shot to be on that ship when it takes off. Whatever I have to do, even if I have to hurt, maim," he swallowed, "*kill* for that to happen, I'll do it. Swear to God."

Meyer grinned, "Good! Reference to the almighty aside, I appreciate your…'can-doedness,'"

Joe frowned.

"But I *am* disappointed that you'd aim so low, Joseph. Here you are, in the finest villa in the entire complex, an area that few even know exists, and you're asking for a *chance*? A *shot*?

"Do you think so little of me? That I'll pay off some file clerk to get your boy clean and back in the lottery? My dear Joseph, what I'm offering you is a guaranteed *seat* on *Minerva*."

Joe furrowed his brow, "How is that *possible*? It's a lottery!" He hid his anger beneath his confusion.

Smitts turned toward his heavies in mock surprise, "Oh, I *apologize*, people, I forgot—it's a lottery!"

The assembled crowd allowed themselves a hearty laugh.

"Joseph, do you actually *believe* that the Powers That Be, that delightfully theatrical President Aguilar and her cronies, would allow something as important as the future of the human race to be decided by pure *chance*?"

Joe steadied his eyes and ground his teeth, "What're you sayin', exactly?"

"I'm saying that the lottery's fixed. It's rigged. In addition to 'the List,' the one with all of the scientists and athletes and great thinkers and those *delightful* foremen who had to have a seat to boss you around for the last three years make sure that you didn't sabotage *their* ridiculous spaceship, all this lottery *is* is a secondary List, one that was determined long, long ago."

"You're *lying*," Joe's head spun. Could it be possible? Could this all be a setup, a way to get millions of forced laborers, all toiling day-after-day for two pre-selected groups? No chance for most to make it on the ship, regardless of what they had been told?

Smitts laughed, "I assure you, I most certainly am not."

"But how—"

Smitts waved the question away before Joe even finished, "How they choose who goes is immaterial. Those who've been selected don't even know that they have been, so to them, they'll just think that they're 'lucky.' That they somehow are 'inferior' to those already on the first List. It's a ready-made caste system, *in space!*"

Meyer waved theatrically at the air, and drew a few laughs from the crowd. He brought the chalice to his lips once more, then grimaced as he found it empty and snapped his fingers. Immediately, a woman rushed over toward him with a silver pitcher with more wine and refilled his obscene goblet. As she did so, Smitts chuckled.

"Fortunately for you, because of my 'reputation' among the Powers That Be, this will work to your advantage. While I and the rest of us stay here, in charge of shepherding the flocks of wayward people waiting for their spectacular, imminent demises, your son will have the opportunity to race toward the stars, onward, upward, and all of that b.s.—" he waved away the final point, "—provided, of course, *you* choose to allow him to do so. But I assume that for you, it's a mere formality."

"What's the catch?" Joe asked.

"Ah, yes, the *catch*," Meyer paced toward the hulking ex-linebacker, "like I said, I'll need an inner circle that can keep the peace once *Minerva's* gone. Strong people, determined people, people of," he shot a glance over at the motley crew of rough-and-tumble bikers and flawlessly-attractive airheads, "high character."

Joe nodded.

"I can get your boy on that ship, but in exchange, you will swear an undying oath of loyalty to me, for the rest of your life."

"Is that all?" Joe asked with an arched eyebrow.

Meyer grinned, "Of course, the work won't exactly be raising *cute wittwle* puppies and catching rainbows in a bottle."

The spectators guffawed.

Smitts stood tall, willing his size to match Joe's frame as he spoke, eyes narrowed and set, "I'm not gonna' lie, some of the things you'll have to do in my employ will shake you to your core, will make you *beg* to be shoveling uranium back in the mines. But you *will* do them. Whatever I say. No questions asked. For the rest...of...*your*...LIFE!"

The final few words were an unearthly hiss, a low reminder of just how Meyer Smitts had rapidly and ruthlessly ascended to the apex of this odd underworld.

Joe took a step forward. He looked down at Meyer, eyes as even as he could keep them, though they still burned through their target.

"You listen to me, Meyer, and you listen good. I am a man of my word, and I'm willin' to make that oath to you. Quite frankly, I don't give half a *damn* about anything right now aside from gettin' my boy on that starship out there. If you can make it happen, my hands are yours."

Meyer allowed his intensity to linger for one second…two. The cowboy reached for the stinger stick at his side as Smitts met Joe's measured glare, watt for watt.

Abruptly, the smile returned to Smitts's face.

"Splendid! Splendid, my dear Joseph. Oh, you *have* made the right decision."

Joe nodded, even though every cell in his body told him that he hadn't.

"Now about your boy. Fortunately, Dr. Figgenbaum," he nodded at the middle-aged woman with the dyed-red hair, "has assured me that she has the tools to both cure any lingering effects of the virus and effectively mask the antibodies that have been created in the boy's bloodstream. All she needs is a vial of blood from a dormant host subject."

Dr. Figgenbaum excused herself from her two dim-witted attendants and produced a syringe from her pocket. She approached Joe, needle-first.

Joe reflexively rolled up his right sleeve, "I had the virus. I'm the one who gave it to him."

Figgenbaum held up her free hand, "Sadly, you are not a *dormant* host. Dormant, for our purposes, means someone who has been symptom-free for over a month."

Joe's head raced. His hand reached involuntarily toward his pocket and fumbled around, past his ID and keys. He pinched his fingers together even as Smitts opened his mouth to speak.

"Does the name Wyatt Port mean anything to you?"

Joe grasped the ring and held it, the metal cool against his burning palm. He willed his face still.

Meyer grinned, "Come now, Joseph. If we're going to do business together, I need to know, with great certainty, that you're on *my* side. That you'll do *anything* I ask."

Joe tilted his head. As annoying as Wyatt could be at times, he was still his *friend*. Like he had already told Meyer, betrayal wasn't a concept he took lightly.

Still, a little harmless conversation couldn't hurt Wyatt, could it?

"I know him," Joe nodded. "On my crew. Big football fan. Loves hearin' my stories about the 'good ol' days.'"

Meyer's lips went thin and serpentine, "What if I told you that Wyatt not only was the perfect *dormant* host, but that he currently occupies the last spot on the second list?"

Joe raised an eyebrow, "What about it?"

"*You're* the first alternate. Which means that, should Wyatt not make it to the launch, and you name young Mason your surrogate," he paused and smiled, "well, you can see what I'm getting at."

"You said you could *guarantee* Mason a spot!" Joe took a step toward Meyer. Two of the bikers, a man and a no-nonsense-looking woman, reached for their stinger sticks.

"And I *am*, should you run this little errand for me, and prove your loyalty to the cause. Wyatt Port currently has the key to your son's life coursing through his veins. He also skimmed off the top of a delivery he made to an associate of mine."

"Wyatt worked for *you*?" Joe asked.

Meyer nodded, "He *also* did some rather sloppy work in roughing up a couple of miners who owed me gambling debts. Got the guards poking around, *very* unprofessional."

Joe didn't move a muscle.

"All you have to do is get a blood sample from him the night before the lottery, and inject him with a sedative to ensure he misses the lottery. When the scanners don't pick him up entering the Grand Hall in the morning, your name gets called instead of him, and," his lips curled upward, "daddy saves the day for young Mason, allowing him to go on a trip to the stars, and most importantly, get off this *rock* before that damned rogue planet annihilates it!"

Joe studied Smitts's eyes, which had become maniacal, yet measured through the course of his monologue. The former linebacker sniffed in a deep lungful of the wonderful, sweet air and let it linger on his nostrils for a moment.

He didn't *need* this weird, hedonistic, downright bacchanalian lifestyle, though part of him ached with yearning for it. It had been too long since he had even a sip of booze, outlawed in Starship City. Longer still since he had felt the soft touch of a woman, as well as that extra beat in his heart that accompanied it, but he could go without it for two more short years.

What it came down to was a vow he had taken those many years ago, after another time in his life that Meyer Smitts had intervened and promised him the world.

A vow that was at odds with an equally solemn promise to get his boy on the ship that stood mere miles away that he mumbled to himself as the two crossed the desert toward this damned city.

Even if that meant betraying his best friend.

Joe's eyes dropped in their sockets. He released the ring in his pocket and nodded.

"I'll do it."

Smitts nodded with a wide grin, "Excellent! Excellent, Joseph!" he clapped his hands twice.

The man in the cowboy hat took several strides toward the pair. He reached for the brushed metal cylinder at his side.

Joe raised his hands in front of his face in a boxing position. The look of grim determination on the cowboy's face was pure grit, equal parts John Wayne and Clint Eastwood. Joe waited, weight balanced on the balls of his feet as the cowboy pulled the stinger stick from his belt.

He flipped it around, handle toward Joe.

"I think you'll be needing this…" he said.

NINE

Joe did his best to hide his limp as he staggered down the hallway, sticking to the brushed metal walls as best as he could to evade any wandering eyes. Curfew had been pushed back until 1 a.m., a mere eight minutes away. And though Joe was making good time, he worried that whomever Meyer sent wouldn't make it.

As he passed each doorway, Wyatt's screams and pleas for mercy tore through Joe's head. Did Wyatt know that he had his ticket punched? That he was on the second List? Was that part of the deal with Smitts? And if so, why should Joe trust Smitts when he simply hung Wyatt out to dry like unspun laundry when the man had disappointed him?

The stinger stick swung against Joe's thigh, still warm from use. He shuddered; whenever his eyelids shut, he was back Wyatt's apartment, bringing the damned awful device down on his friend, watching as Wyatt sizzled and seized, not relenting until he was sure he had passed out.

There had to have been another way, Joe thought.

He knew there wasn't; what else *could* he have done? Wyatt got the jump on *him.* Bit *him.* Left him no choice.

You didn't have to be so cruel!

"How the hell not!?" Joe hissed. He wiped his face as he cursed himself; even if he was tired, it was careless to say anything so close to curfew. If Smitts *did* deliver, he wanted to make sure that Mason's ticket wasn't forfeited.

He rounded the right-hand curve of the hallway, the final stretch before their apartment, and noticed once more that the gleaming, polished windows and railings had already lost their luster, and were beginning to film over and dull.

If it's like this already, and Minerva *hasn't even lifted off, what'll it be like tomorrow once it's gone?* Joe thought.

A few short days before, he would have shuddered at the thought. Now, though, he welcomed whatever punishment this place thought it proper to bestow upon him. After all, wasn't that what he signed up for when he decided to go into business with Meyer Smitts?

The freshly-dilapidated hallway straightened, and Joe found his answer.

Dr. Figgenbaum herself stood in his doorway, dressed in standard maintenance crew coveralls with the saccharinely-hopeful "SSC" logo stenciled on the front, along with a name in tiny white print.

"Doctor…Winters, I presume?" Joe deadpanned, surveying the name on her chest.

Rancid breath leaked through unbrushed teeth as Figgenbaum unleashed a soft cackle.

"Meyer *said* you'd be a good sport about all of this. Makes me feel like a bit of a spy, traipsing around under cover of darkness, conducting," she brought her hand up to shield her mouth, "*illicit business* in plain sight. What a thrill!"

Unfortunately, her hand only had the effect of guiding her foul-smelling breath toward Joe's face.

He endured it, grimly.

"Do you have the sample?" she asked.

Joe reached in his pocket, into the spot formerly occupied by his Rose Bowl ring, and pulled out the vial of dark, cloudy liquid.

"Excellent!" Figgenbaum clasped her hands together with glee. She took out a device little larger than a holophone and inserted the small container into the holographic fitting it projected. Lights flashed and the phone let out a low hum.

"I don't know *why* it does that," Figgenbaum said. "One'a the fastest computers ever made, and it can't handle a little on-the-fly gene sequencing and replication!"

Joe snorted, even though he failed to see the humor of the joke.

The light turned green, and Figgenbaum removed the vial. She replaced it with a similar, empty vessel, and tapped another button on the holodisplay.

Within seconds, Joe was astonished to find the vial filling rapidly with bright green liquid.

His mouth hung unhinged as the light turned green once more. Figgenbaum removed the little plastic jar and replaced it with another. After she topped off the second container with the fluorescent fluid, she inserted a small fitting on the end of each vial and flipped them to the confused former linebacker.

"All done!" she beamed. "Just insert the pointy end into your neck and your boy's neck within the hour, and you'll both have a clean bill of health come boarding time tomorrow."

"But how did it—?"

Figgenbaum cackled again, "I like you, kid," Joe half expected her to pinch his cheek, even though she was only maybe a dozen years his senior. Instead, she rose to her tip-toes and patted him awkwardly on his chest, "We're gonna' do fine here together...*just* fine..."

She stretched out a wrinkled, rubbery hand and turned her gaze to Joe's belt.

Joe thought the middle-aged woman was making a pass at him.

Then he realized the stinger stick still hung at his side. He removed it and handed it over to the doctor; no need to keep the damning evidence anywhere near his apartment. She collected it with a wry grin.

Joe shook his head as the woman put her pointer finger to her lips.

"SHHHH!" she hissed too-loudly in the empty hallway.

Joe cringed.

Figgenbaum's grimy teeth flashed through the dim light.

"Have a good night—see you tomorrow!" She waved a stilted "goodbye," and clomped down the hallway, curfew be damned.

Joe shook his head and allowed a muted smile despite the evening's events. Though Joe found her acrid breath repulsive, there was something charming about the woman in a mad-scientist sort of way, that disarmed him a bit, and made him forget, if only momentarily, about the situation he had put his friend in.

He shut one eye and looked at the fitting Figgenbaum had placed on the end of the vial. It was a curious contraption, a nanoneedle housed in some sort of casing, presumably to even out pressure on the skin and prevent the usual pinch that accompanied such inoculations.

Joe didn't hesitate; he wanted to make sure Smitts and Figgenbaum weren't conspiring to hurt or kill both Grissoms, so he quickly jammed one of the vials into his own neck, an eager guinea pig.

He felt a sharp pinch for a moment that nearly made him cry out in pain, but Joe bit his lip and bore through it.

He waited ten seconds…twenty…thirty. When the clock mounted in the hallway changed to "12:59," and he still felt fine, he nodded. He took a deep breath and blew it out slowly.

He paused and took two pained strides over to the window next to the door, and peered upward.

Hanging in the night sky, as always, was Destiny, angry, red, and growing in size by the night. Though Joe hadn't been able to gauge the progression from "pin-prick of light" to "blazing red hole punched in the heavens," it wasn't nearly as big as the moon yet; that's when all of the scientists said they would know the end was close. Still, Joe found it oddly comforting to survey the arbiter of their doom, uncaring as it may be, if only to quiet the throes of his own bruised conscience.

Joe shook his head as he stumbled over to the apartment's door. He inserted the key in the lock of his apartment and turned it, which caused the door to open. The only light came from the holovision set, which was close to shutting itself off for the evening.

"Reports of last-minute stowaways on *Minerva* being removed from Starship City and executed have, thus, been *greatly* exaggerated," the female anchor said with a smile. She tapped her thin tablet on the desk in front of her, "And with that, I must say it's been my distinct *honor* to deliver the news to you each and every evening during our three year journey. I hope to see many of you in the halls of *Minerva* in the coming years, and look forward to getting to know each and every one of you. This is Dana Teagan, SSC News, signing off."

A montage of patriotic images filled the room alongside the constant, looming presence of *Minerva,* and was accompanied by an orchestral rendition of "America the Beautiful."

Joe hummed the final few lines softly and ironically, shaking his head all the while. He hoped to gently wake Mason from his sprawled slumber on the sofa.

Mason responded by turning over and pulling the comforter over his head.

Joe took a seat on an unoccupied part of the couch and put his hand on his son's shoulder.

"You and I both know you aren't gettin' any sleep right now," Joe said.

"Doesn't hurt to try," Mason said. He pulled the blanket off his head, revealing dark circles under his bloodshot eyes, "'specially when I know I'm not gettin' on *Minerva* tomorrow."

He rolled over to face his father.

For the first time all evening, Joe couldn't help but grin. He reached into his pocket and produced the bright green vial that Figgenbaum provided him.

"What's that?" Mason asked. "Drugs?"

Joe frowned, "No. No, not *drugs*! What the *hell* kinda' father you think I am?"

"Eh, a pretty good one," Mason deadpanned.

"Somethin' tells me you're gonna' upgrade your assessment once I tell ya' what this is."

Joe took a deep breath. He flicked the side of the vial a couple of times as the bright green liquid shone in the darkness, "*That* is medicine. Special medicine. It's gonna' fix ya' up, make it so that the scanners can't tell that you're sick."

Mason rubbed his eyes before he realized what his father had said and they went wide. He reached for the vial at first out of curiosity, a curiosity soon replaced by greed as he recognized what it represented.

Joe pulled it back.

"Give it here!" Mason pleaded. "Come on, Dad. Give it here!"

"Hold your horses!" Joe smiled. "I just have to sort of, uh, inject it."

Mason didn't flinch as he held out an arm.

"In your neck."

Mason didn't say a word and craned his neck away from Joe, giving his dad a larger target to hit.

"Do it," Mason commanded, his voice firm and deep.

Joe nodded with pride. He gripped the tiny vial in his huge hand and brought it, point-first, toward his son's skin.

"It ain't supposed to hurt," Joe said as he swiftly closed the distance, and stuck his son in the neck.

Mason didn't move a muscle as the nanoneedle found its mark. Joe watched as the fluid drained rapidly into his son's neck, hopefully giving him the promise of a life to which neither of them currently could lay claim.

For the briefest of moments, Joe allowed a sinister thought to creep into his head:

What if Smitts double-crossed me? What if this was meant for show? Or what if it was some kind of latent poison? The possibilities started to lodge themselves in Joe's mind.

Joe dismissed the voice with a shake of his head. Crazy as she may be, Figgenbaum was still a doctor, and that meant she had taken an oath to do no harm.

Yeah, Destiny's gonna' do plenty…for everyone, Joe thought again.

If the serum was meant to cause Mason harm, he didn't show any ill-effects.

"Dad?" Mason asked.

"Yeah son?"

"I know, I mean, you always tell me not to get my hopes up, and I get that, but I don't think I ever thanked you for going through all this. All of the hard work and everything, just so we'd have a shot to be together on *Minerva*."

Joe forced a grim smile. It was okay for Mason to believe that for now—anything to get him through tonight, through tomorrow, onto that ship.

Joe nodded, "You'll do something similar for your boy someday. I promise."

Mason wrapped his long, thin arms around his father's massive torso and drew himself close.

Joe didn't waste any time in reciprocating; he wrapped his son in a huge, hearty bear hug, though both men stifled the tears that threatened to leak from their eyes. Joe's massive, bruised hands, still sticky with remnants of Wyatt's blood, cradled the boy's head and neck.

They held each other that way for minutes, well past the point of comfort for both, each terrified to let go lest the other slip away unnoticed into the darkness.

TEN

The lines were massive, three-fourths of the way down each hallway in the sprawling, five-armed, spiral-shaped structure that comprised Starship City.

At the end of each queue was the Grand Hall, a large, majestic room the size of dozens of enormous airplane hangars. It was situated at a suitable altitude to allow the large, reinforced windows to frame a view of the *Minerva*, polished and ready to go. The Hall had previously housed the offices of various scientists, planners, and leaders that were on the List, and thus already had a seat on the ship. It was telling that both a hallway and a monorail ran directly from the Grand Hall to the ship's gangway, a mile away, just in case anything had gone wrong through the construction process.

On Lottery Day, no matter what a person's position, from the most brilliant scientist on down to the sleaziest bureaucrat who had wormed his way onto the ship through lies and double-dealing, every member of the List had some duty to process the millions of inhabitants of Starship City as they marched through the complex.

Many were assigned to security detail, and held their stinger sticks in tremulous hands, already alight with tiny blue bolts that sizzled between the end prongs. Armed with one of the awful devices, even the slightest-framed scientist with a stooped back could, theoretically, subdue someone of Joe's imposing size.

The happy-looking, green-eyed scannerbots roamed the hallways spouting hopelessly optimistic platitudes.

"Congratulations!"

"Way to go!"

"We did it!"

Joe figured it was best to ignore all of the ramifications of the next few hours, not only for themselves, but for the entirety of the human race. Instead, he whiled away the minutes by asking Mason about movies.

"No way, Dad—*Omicron Zero* is the *best* movie *ever*!"

"I don't know—that Jayden Smith was great when he was winning Oscars back in the day, but I just don't buy him as a wise-crackin' old man."

"That's the point!" Mason exclaimed.

Before they knew it, the two passed through the autoscanners mounted above the doors to the first holding area. As they passed underneath, the machines covered them with rays of pale blue light. Nearly instantaneously, their pictures were projected from the holodisplays next to the entrance.

A lukewarm, feminine voice greeted them.

"Welcome Joseph Robert Grissom. You are approved to enter."

"Welcome Mason Liam Grissom. You are approved to enter."

Their pictures flashed briefly before they were replaced by those of the people behind them.

Mason looked at his father, eyes wide with hope.

Joe shook his head, *That's not the big one,* he thought. He nodded at the next set of doors, with a simultaneously friendly, ominous yellow sign that read "Preliminary Medical Check."

Mason's eyes went wider. He swallowed deeply as Joe subconsciously placed a huge paw on his son's back.

That's not the big one, either, he thought. Though it was true that the Powers That Be would conduct a final, individual scan on everyone before they were allowed to head over to *Minerva*, Joe thought that this first checkpoint would at least be some indication of whether Figgenbaum's concoction was worth the price he paid.

Or will pay, Joe thought.

The yellow light washed over them as they approached the doorway.

"Please exhale," the same female voice emplored them.

Joe and Mason let out hearty sighs as they exchanged glances.

The scanner took a half-second to process the results.

"Please continue," it said, without any emotion.

Joe sighed again as Mason smiled.

"Dad, it—"

Before they had taken five steps, red lights flashed and sirens blared. Grey shirts rushed toward them, stinger sticks already out and ready.

Joe stood his ground, hunched, and ready to fight. He waited as the grey shirts approached, eyes set with grim determination, jogging toward them…toward them…toward them…

…And past them.

The grey shirts picked a pale-looking fortiesh woman out of line, her bleary eyes open and trembling in their heavy sockets, skin yellowed and clammy.

"Warning: pathogen detected!" The voice alerted the crowd. "Dispensing countermeasures."

The area was enveloped by a thick, ozone-smelling fog. Joe straightened as he craned his neck to see the fate of the woman behind him, but the mist was too thick. When he heard a sharp scream, followed by the ghastly whine of the stinger sticks being deployed on their target, and a barely-audible "thud," Joe didn't need to see anything else.

His head reeled; how long had she been back there, unnoticed? The fog was supposed to kill any and all bacteria, but what if she had sneezed in line? What if they had already been contaminated?

Joe pondered this fresh hell as he guided Mason along with his hand. He didn't even stop as the two locked eyes. This time, Joe offered his son a reassuring nod.

"It's okay. It'll all be fine," Joe said, his eyes forward again.

They continued through several ante-rooms, each with various security countermeasures designed to detect homemade explosives, weapons, and other contraband, until only one entrance remained. They cleared that final barrier, and were guided by flashing holographic lights on the ground to join others in strict, clean rows of people, separated into roughly square sections by larger aisles. Lines upon lines of weary workers and their families that filled the massive structure as grey shirts patrolled between them.

The room was even more expansive than Joe had heard it described.

"This thing must be a hundred football fields," he said to Mason, before he reconsidered, "Maybe a *thousand*."

"It's *huge!*" Mason echoed his father.

Soothing valedictory music played over the loudspeakers, as pithy platitudes were splashed in occasionally.

"Congratulations!" "*We* did it!" "Outstanding!"

At the front of the room, banners were hung: "Congratulations Starship City!" "The Human Race Thanks *You!*"

Joe snorted. He could barely shake his head as so many hopeful faces allowed themselves to be roped in to the spectacle. Smiles and laughs that would vaporize in just a few more minutes.

Followed by the planet in a couple years, Joe thought.

The mass of humanity continued to file into the enormous facility, into their neat rows, wrangled by the ominous, low hum of ready stinger sticks wielded by grey shirts. The lone exception was a stage near the tunnel and monorail stop at the front of the room, heavily guarded by at least two rows of grey shirts, stinger sticks out and ready.

Occasionally, a scanner darted above them, its unblinking, green eye surveying the crowd for any security threats, and, Joe imagined, logging in each person's name and location to develop a map the Powers That Be could use for the lottery.

After several more minutes, a series of loud "CLANG"s from around the edge of the room jolted him, and sent the rest of the crowd into a round of muted hysterics.

The Grand Hall went dark momentarily before a spotlight shone onto the stage at the front of the cavernous space. Inside the beam was a short, stocky middle-aged fellow behind a microphone stand, whose image was holoprojected above the stage, as well as in front of each section by a scannerbot.

"Ladies and Gentlemen, the President of the United States!"

The first few bars of "Hail to the Chief" resonated throughout the room. A mocha-skinned woman with a broad smile and practiced wave emerged from the monorail car onto the stage, and took the place of the herald on the display.

Mason clapped loudly along with the rest of the room.

Joe offered three exaggerated, sarcastic clomps with his massive hands.

"Hello, Starship City!" President Aguilar waved to the smiling masses, each person barely able to contain their outright glee.

"Has it been three years already?" She forced a laugh, her gleaming white teeth leading the chorus of world-weary former miners, smelters, and finishers.

"We've been through a lot, haven't we? Russian and Chinese sneak attacks," boos filled the room, "brutal work schedules, little sleep. And it's not just you; my staff and I have been working tirelessly around-the-clock to ensure that *Minerva* was a success. It's been a team effort, and a team victory, not just for these United States of America, but for the entirety of the human race!"

Another loud spate of cheers.

I wonder if her shoulder's getting tired from patting herself on the back? Joe thought.

She motioned for the crowd to quiet down, "It was only decades ago that ordinary folks thought that we were testing alien spaceships about a hundred miles that way," she pointed to her right, "at a place called Area 51."

The room erupted in derisive laughter.

"See? Everyone in the room believes such a concept to be absurd!" she focused her eyes on the back of the room, "yet now, *we* have a chance to be those very same aliens landing on someone else's planet. Hoping to appeal to the same sense of justice and peace with which we would have welcomed other forms of life with open arms, should we have had the chance to encounter them here on Earth, our old home."

Polite applause rose from the masses.

Aguilar's smile dropped as her lip quivered, "Of course, not all of us will be able to embark on the voyage to humanity's new home. Remember, regardless of the outcome of the lottery today, you should *all* be proud of your service to your country and your species. How 'bout a big round of applause for everyone in here who worked on the project? List members, too—I know you can clap around those stinger sticks!"

This round of clapping was more methodical and mechanical. Joe found it telling that despite the President's urging, none of the grey shirts dared to drop their guard.

Aguilar flashed her blinding smile once more, "And now, for the business of the day!" she waved a hand over her head, and her picture disappeared from the various displays as the space in front of the huge windows at the front of the room came alive with color and motion. The swirling shapes and forms eventually separated out into a cartoonish, oversized, sign that read, "THE LOTTERY!" in all caps.

Joe couldn't help but notice the American flag that waved behind the words, nor could he ignore the majestic bald eagle that would occasionally swoop in front of the letters.

Many in the crowd whooped and cheered with delight, though the number of people who clutched loved ones or held their heads in their hands had increased markedly.

"As you know, the lottery is separated into three rounds of four thousand selections each. The selections will occur simultaneously, and chosen individuals will be illuminated by our wonderful scannerbots flying around the room.

"If you are chosen, stay put. Members of our security staff will find you and escort you to the tunnel at the front of the room, where you'll be individually scanned and placed into the ship's computer. Each cadre of individuals chosen will then make the short trek to *Minerva* through the tunnel behind me to my right, your left, at the front of the room."

Aguilar nodded over her shoulder.

"At the end of the third round, we have a very special treat for you, so be sure to stay put and listen—you *aren't* going to want to miss this one!"

Joe and Mason eyed each other skeptically.

"So without further ado, please remain calm as we begin the lottery. Remember, violators of the Starship City code of conduct will be incapacitated or removed from the premises in accordance with 56 U.S.C. 1117."

Two grey shirts wheeled a giant red lever across the stage to the President. A nervous hum fell on the crowd.

Mason grabbed a handful of Joe's enormous fingers.

Joe brought his other arm around to Mason's shoulder and pulled him in tight.

President Aguilar took three graceful steps over to the lever. She grabbed the handle with both hands and pulled with surprising force.

Immediately, the green eyes on the scannerbots went yellow. Within seconds, the basketball-sized machines darted about the room, turning on a dime and stopping in front of the selected few.

Several rows in front of Joe and Mason, a bot hovered in front of a dark-skinned woman.

"Martina Shales, congratulations, you have been selected in the *Minerva* lottery," the same, robotic voice from the anteroom scanners deadpanned.

"Oh my God…oh my *God*! Praise Jesus!" the woman yelled, her tone wavering with relief.

Joe craned his neck to get a look at her. Attractive. In her mid-thirties. Maybe in another life he would have bumped into her at a supermarket and asked for her phone number.

Fits Smitts's profile so far, Joe said.

The vastness of the room was underscored by the relative lack of selections in their general vicinity. Hopeful smiles turned to measured frowns as people began to realize just how thin their odds were, and exactly how many hours, how many weeks, how many *years* of labor they had put in for this fleeting moment.

Even at this early stage of the lottery, Joe heard several isolated whines of stinger sticks being deployed on unruly astronaut hopefuls, ending their chances at being selected.

Keep it together, Joe, he thought. *You didn't come all this way, do what you've done, to be smacked outta' line by some damned grey shirt. If that's the case, may as well've been shot in line back in the desert three years ago*, he thought.

This thought was followed quickly by, *Speak of the devils*, as thousands of grey shirts hustled the first round of the lucky thousands through the thin aisles and toward the front of the room. An area had been cleared next to the stage filled with scannerbots, which rapidly processed the health and genetic profiles of those passing through, and quickly gave a green "yes" or red "no" light.

Joe watched as hundreds of flashing "greens" went off, one after another as the winners gave various fist-pumps and howls of celebration. They ascended the stage and ran into the tunnels, afraid that someone would tap them on the shoulder and inform them of a "clerical error" at any moment.

It was an efficient business; in all, the first round took only fifteen minutes or so. Joe was impressed.

The Nazis were efficient, too, you know, he thought.

Joe scowled at the critical voice in his head. He forced it to the periphery.

It's fine. *He'll be* fine, Joe thought.

The President stepped up to the mike, "Round Two!" she said with a coy, almost seductive smile broadcast in a large hologram above her head. She pulled the ceremonial lever again. The scannerbots came back to life. Joe noticed a trickle of grey shirts slowly following the first group down the tunnel.

This time, even as the scannerbots coasted to-and-fro, announcing the next round of 4,000, Joe actually only saw a grand total of two people selected in their vicinity. One was a girl not much older than Mason, also attractive, eyes bright, alive and intelligent.

"Tenna Jaskevich, congratulations, you have been selected in the *Minerva* lottery," the mechanical female voice said.

The young woman's eyes went wide with shock. She hugged the older man to her left, and the (also fetching, Joe noted) woman to her right as grey shirts hustled to her position.

After several seconds, she realized exactly what "being selected" actually meant. Her vibrant eyes went slick with tears as she tried to hug both mother and father simultaneously.

"Go, Tenna," her father had to try to pry her off him. "It's okay! You made it. We're *proud* of you!" The man said.

Joe looked at Mason, who was taking the scene in.

He hoped he was so lucky to have such a conversation with his son.

The grey shirts grabbed the young woman by the arms and hustled her along the pathway.

"I love you! I LOVE YOU!" she cried.

"We love you, honey!" Mom and Dad yelled back, their voices raspy and weary, yet, Joe thought, appropriately satisfied.

This time, the process went even more quickly, maybe ten minutes in all, though the raw murmur of the increasingly worried denizens of Starship City continued to be punctuated by increasingly frequent, sharp, electronic sounds of stinger sticks brought to bear on troublemakers.

Two sections over, Joe heard a distinct, "They can't take all of us!"

The cacophony of piercing cries and distorted sounds of stinger sticks that followed convinced Joe to the contrary.

He wondered why, after all of the hard work, the forced labor, the awful conditions, the toil and servitude, why anyone would rebel *now*, even with one round to go. He could even see it after the third round: how *would* they deal with all of these angry people left behind to be obliterated? But after the second?

Was it the oppressive sunniness of the constant propaganda that finally crashed down on them in one final tsunami at the end, and caused them to crack? Or was it the now very real notion that they wouldn't be on that ship when it took off in mere minutes?

Once the second round was processed, the President stepped up to the podium once more.

"Alright, everyone, it's time for the third round," a coy smile washed over Aguilar's face, "I didn't say *final* round, now did I? Hmm..." she placed an index finger on the corner of her mouth, subtle as a dinner-theater actor.

A hopeful murmur spread through the crowd like creamy peanut butter on bread.

She seemed to look everyone in the room in the eye as she continued facing forward, and pulled the lever one more time.

The scannerbots launched into action. Joe tried to ignore the buzzing little robots as they flew overhead, but he couldn't help but follow them as they shot to-and-fro about the room.

One of them stopped in front of Joe's section. Joe nodded almost imperceptibly as it scanned the group, and headed straight for him, advancing into the third row, then the fourth. Joe watched as it hovered toward him, the culmination of all of the hard work, the sacrifice, the awful things he had done and was yet to do.

He watched as it continued past him, and settled over a trim, attractive brunette.

"Maya Dreslough, congratulations, you have been selected in the *Minerva* lottery,"

Joe's lip curled into a snarl. He turned and leveled an eye on the woman.

That's my son's *ticket! Smitts* screwed *me!*

He watched as the scannerbots finished their rounds and returned to the stage at the front of the room, as grey shirts hustled winners to the front of the room.

This time, a huge swath of grey shirts preceded the winning cadre down the tunnel toward the ship. They would have to get situated in their stations before liftoff—scheduled for a short half hour from then—could occur.

Enough of the guards stayed behind, though, to tend to each section, stinger sticks mostly raised and at the ready.

"Mostly" raised, except for the petite female grey shirt who stood, facing forward toward the stage, hands grasped behind her back. Joe's eyes focused on the stinger stick that hung tantalizingly by her side. He felt

91

betrayed, by Smitts, by Figgenbaum, hell, even by Aguilar. It would be so easy to push a few people aside, overpower her, take the stinger stick and fight his way onto *Destiny*...

He steadied himself and shifted his weight to the balls of his feet, ready to take that first step out of line, the one that would almost certainly damn him.

I have to try something, he thought.

He picked his right foot up off the ground, ready to pounce on the guard and at least take some of them down with him...

Joe felt a tug on his sleeve.

Mason's piercing eyes stared back at him, the fear washed out of them, unafraid and poised.

"I wonder what the President meant about the surprise here at the end, Dad."

Joe's eyes widened. As soon as his son had finished, he remembered Smitts's exact words:

What if I told you that Wyatt not only was the perfect dormant host, but that he currently occupies the last spot on the second list?

The *last* spot. Maybe, just maybe, Mason still had a chance. Joe nodded at his son and turned his attention to the front of the room.

The crowd grew impatient as Aguilar held two fingers to her ear, waiting for the go-ahead from *Minerva* to begin the final round.

Another twenty minutes passed. The crowd grew restless. Ocassionally, the whine of a stinger stick followed by a sharp cry pierced the din of the impatient masses.

Finally, Aguilar nodded and stepped up to the microphone.

"Well, everyone, I *do* apologize for the delay, but we have one final order of business to attend to. Actually, we have several. Firstly, the government of the United States of America would like to thank you for your loyal service, regardless of what happens from this point forward. To that end, we have assembled refreshment stations containing your favorite alcoholic and non-alcoholic beverages, as well as appetizers and desserts, around the edges of the room as a big 'thank you' to all of you who have given up so much to be here."

The President clapped loudly for herself into the microphone, as did the grey shirts flanking the stage.

The only other noises in the room were muffled groans of sarcastic indignation.

Aguilar raised a palm toward the crowd, "In addition!" she raised her voice to quiet the rising tide of outbursts. Another stinger stick went off. Then another. "In addition, we have one final lottery winner for the last spot on the ship."

She let the sentiment hang over the room for several moments.

The stinger sticks went silent.

Aguilar grinned, "One last selection who will have the honor of accompanying the remaining members of the List, including me, on the Presidential monorail to embark on *Minerva*."

The groans and jeers turned to hopeful, rising hums and "oh"s.

"So it is my great honor and privilege to *thank* you, one more time, and with one final pull of the lever, I will bid you all adieu. Farewell, good luck, God *bless* America, and God *bless Earth!*"

The swirling, colorful holographics above the stage sprung to life once more. Aguilar quickly pulled the lever and the scannerbots came to life. Grey shirts surrounded the President and rushed her into the front car of the waiting monorail.

A contingent of two-dozen grey shirts jogged down the hallways. By their steely jaws and the purpose in their strides, Joe could've sworn they already knew where they were going.

He thought it was a masterful plan on the part of the President and her staff: hustle most of the guards off to the ship ahead of time, have her waiting and ready to go in the monorail, process the final winner quickly and with a minimum of hassle, and take off before the troublemakers could force their way through to the ship.

The scannerbots flew in long, wide arcs around the room, giving hope to all those in attendance as the grey shirts stalked their target largely unnoticed. The flying robots would stop at various intervals, giving the members of a section false hope before moving on to another one.

Joe watched and waited as one scannerbot buzzed overhead, followed by another. The grey shirts were headed up the rows, moving over horizontally every so often, putting them on a diagonal toward their target.

They stopped in formation, two lines of a dozen or so grey shirts each, right in front of Joe's section. Each line peeled off into a tight arc as the grey shirts worked their way through the crowd, not hesitating to swing or poke at the people in Joe's section with stinger sticks should the crowd pause even for a moment.

Mason's eyes went wide—he tapped his father on the elbow and pointed at the gathering crowd of scannerbots floating above their section. As the grey shirts cut through the first several rows in front of them, the robots bathed Joe in soft green light.

"Joseph Grissom, congratulations, you have been selected in the *Minerva* lottery,"

ELEVEN

July 21, 2066
T-Minus 15 minutes

What happened next seemed to be in slow motion. The grey shirts took up positions flanking Joe. He grabbed Mason tight, and gave them no option but to surround the boy, as well.

"Hang on!" Joe yelled.

The crowd turned vile. Lacking weapons, they took off their shoes and began casting them at Joe, Mason, and the grey shirts. The grey shirts responded by swinging stinger sticks wildly at anyone in their path, moving like Roman Legionaries with calm, confident steps toward the front of the room.

These grey shirts were clearly pros; full-time security forces, not moonlighting scientists or bureaucrats.

Joe and Mason were caught up in the tide. One piece of footwear caught its mark, hitting Joe squarely on the forehead. Joe's eyes narrowed at the annoyance.

"Dad? Dad, what's this mean? Don't *leave* me, Dad!" Mason cried.

Joe responded by throwing a massive elbow over the boy's head, shielding him from any of the projectiles launched his way.

Survival instinct kicked in; the same poor fools that Joe had pitied mere moments before were now enemies standing in his way, *Mason's* way, to the front of the room, to that last ticket.

Once they reached the aisle, a cool shadow washed over Joe's head. The scannerbots had assembled in a circular formation above them, and mimicked the movements of the grey shirts.

The mob grew angrier, emboldened. Even two dozen grey shirts would be hard-pressed to deal with the million-or-so left behind on their own.

Which is why Joe was surprised, but not shocked by what he saw next:

The scannerbots, those peaceable heralds of hope, the friendly faces that greeted so many people onto *Minerva* minutes earlier, lit up with flashes of pale, green light. Laser volleys flew into the crowd in front of the group, carving out a path toward the stage.

Joe didn't even pause to see the hole-ridden corpses strewn about. The grey shirts picked up speed as those who failed to get out of the way were either stung and cast aside or mowed down by the unrelenting scannerbots.

By the end, they had broken into a full sprint. Joe grabbed Mason's arm and refused to let go, carrying the teenager to the front of the room.

A lone, friendly scannerbot waited behind a wall of grey shirts, furiously beating back the crowd. The guards parted to allow Joe and Mason through.

A grey shirt, whose crooked nose supported thin, stylish glasses over tight, grim eyes, greeted them.

"Joseph?" he asked.

"I voluntarily cede my spot to my son, Mason," Joe said.

The grey shirt nodded.

Mason's eyes went wide, "Dad? You can't—you won the spot. You gotta' go, Dad!"

"You were sayin' I can't leave you a few minutes ago!"

"I'm still sayin' it *now*!" Mason yelled. "I'd rather be with you, here. Even if it's only two more years."

Joe placed a massive hand on each of his son's shoulders, "You listen to me, and you listen good. This, all of this," he rolled his head around the room for effect, "it's gone. It's doomed. Gonna' be damned *dust*. You get on that ship—you knew this was the plan from the start if I—" he paused and chewed the final word, "—*won*."

"Now that it's here, though—"

"Now that it's here," Joe gritted his teeth, "You do me proud, you raise your own family, and you carry on the Grissom name with honor. Honor that *I* could never give it."

His stare bore into his son's eyes, deep past the pupils, probing him, forcing him to see *reason*.

"Please, son," the wrinkles around Joe's eyes grew pronounced, "do it for me."

"Kind of need an answer here, folks," the grey shirt pressed them.

Joe shot him a measured glare filled with the three years of awful treatment he had endured.

The grey shirt's eyes widened, "I'll, uh, give you two a minute."

Mason looked back at his father. Joe couldn't help but smile at the young man. He saw the vitality and youth, all of the strength and courage that Joe lacked when he looked in the mirror at Wyatt's place those few hours ago.

The teenager nodded.

"Okay. I'll do it," Mason raised a skeptical eye toward the individual scanner.

The nervous grey shirt clenched his teeth together, "Great. Eyes toward the scanner and exhale."

The bot washed Mason in green light. He puffed out his cheeks and held the breath in for an extra beat before releasing it. Joe knew that the scan was quick and routine, but in his mind, it seemed like an eternity, each half-second an interminable form of torture as he waited to see if Smitts and Figgenbaum had held up their side of the bargain.

The scannerbot's eye stood, yellow in its indecisive judgment. Part of Joe thought the damned thing would surely go nuts and start firing lasers at them an minute, as its bretheren now did to hold off those brave (or foolish) enough to try to storm the monorail and tunnel to the ship.

The yellow orb around its electronic eye turned. Joe wanted to say that it was thinking, but he knew it was merely processing data it had collected, was going through subroutines and analyzing atoms. This machine, this *device* would be the final arbiter of his son's fate.

The eye went green.

"Fantastic. Welcome aboard," the grey shirt pushed his glasses up on his face, already hustling to the monorail.

The lines of grey shirts closed ranks, retreating toward the monorail car.

Mason looked at his father. Joe met his gaze.

Without warning, the teenager threw his arms around his father as Joe fell to a knee. A single teardrop hung perilously from the elder Grissom's eyelid.

"I love you, Dad. Thank you." Mason couldn't hold back the tide of his own sobs any longer.

"I love you more than life itself," Joe said. He pulled away from the embrace and put his hands on the boy's shoulder's once more, "And I'll do anything, *anything*, to find you again before I die."

Mason nodded gravely. He wanted to stay there, safe in his father's arms, even though he knew that nothing was safe anymore, not even *Minerva*.

Joe gave his son a gentle push toward the Monorail as the grey shirts backed up to him.

"Go. *Go!*" Joe said.

One of the greyshirts turned and bolted for the monorail. Another one flew past, though this one grabbed Mason on his way. The teenager got one last look at his father, one more glance at the man who now rose to his feet.

Joe nodded and sighed. It had cost him everything: his friend. His life.

His *soul*.

But as Mason got on board the monorail with the remaining grey shirts, and the crowd stormed the stage, laser bolts flying all around him, Joe Grissom smiled. He allowed himself a hearty sigh, and leaned his head back, the cries of mowed-down others drowned out in his brief reverie.

He was finally content.

TWELVE

July 21, 2066
T-Minus 10 minutes

The final grey shirt aboard hit a button, as the doors shut on the monorail, launching the craft toward *Minerva*, a short mile or so away.

President Aguilar sat in the only seat in the car, flanked by grey shirts. She shook her head, permanently sunny disposition now subsumed beneath a grave, emotionless mask.

"In all my years on this Earth, I never thought I'd have to do something so horrible."

One of the grey shirts, a tall, athletic, Indian man with a square crew-cut shook his head.

"Ma'am, it was all you could do, ma'am."

She nodded grimly, as if trying to convince herself that was the case.

She locked eyes with Mason. At first, he pretended like he hadn't seen her; after all, he'd never see his father again because of her and her *stupid* lottery system.

Instead, he was met with an overbroad smile.

"Well, at least we got such a *handsome* young man as the final selection," she said. "What's your name?"

Mason hoped the intensity of his gaze wasn't lost on her, "Mason. Mason Grissom."

"Well, Mason Grissom, I'm Lupe Aguilar. Nice to meet you."

She reached out a friendly hand, one that he took.

"Excited to be on *Minerva*?"

Mason nodded, unsmiling.

"Well, *that's* good. Certainly better than—"

"All due respect, ma'am, I just lost my father. I'd like to be alone with my thoughts for a while."

Her lips went taut, "Of course. Of course. Take a while—grieving is *certainly* an important part of Stage One."

For now, Mason didn't need to know more. He stood silently as the monorail raced toward the monstrous ship that towered above them, ever-more imposing as they approached it.

Dad worked on this? Mason thought. He had seen it every night out of the window, but even as it towered over Starship City, it always seemed so small, so distant, like it was a ship made for ants more than anything else.

They pulled into the station. Grey shirts formed ranks around President Aguilar, leaving Mason to hustle behind to keep up. A freight elevator operated by two grey shirts was already waiting as the entire party crammed on and was whisked up to the embarkation area.

Bright red railings practically shone off of the polished, brushed metal exterior of the ship. "Loading Zone A" was stenciled on the skin of the craft, as Aguilar and the guards hustled on.

Just as Mason was about to embark, Aguilar stopped and turned. Something about her grin was measured, near-sinister as she waved a hand at him and cleared her throat.

"Yes, ma'am?" Horrible thoughts raced through Mason's mind. What did he do wrong? Were they not even going to let him on the ship? After all he had been through with his father, and—

Aguilar's smile warmed, "Can you hit that button on your way in to close the door?" she asked.

Mason breathed a sigh of relief. He bolted onboard and stood clear of the door as he hit the button. Sirens blared as the massive outer door swung shut, not to be opened again for years.

# # #

Joe stood among the throng as they pushed their way on stage, kept at bay only by the repeated efforts of the scannerbots, even after the monorail had left, and both the monorail track and the tunnel to the ship had been sealed by enormous, heavy blast doors.

I hope he made it, Joe thought. Visions of Wyatt's dream danced in his head. For a moment, he was so overcome by nausea that he nearly retched.

As he looked out toward *Minerva* and thought of all of the hours he spent crafting the thing, he had to admit, it was damned impressive. An achievement that no other civilization, past or current, possibly could have managed. Though their methods, and what he had done, intensified his feelings of illness, he couldn't help but take some twisted pride in having helped to build humanity's crowning achievement.

Then he heard it:

The whine of a stinger stick coming to life.

Then another.

Joe turned and found a coterie of rough-looking men and women flanking none other than Meyer Smitts himself.

They moved swiftly and ruthlessly through the crowd, stinging those who dared to get in their way.

The room grew still and quiet; who *were* these people? Starship City's denizens had grown used to the buttoned-up grey shirts and their ruthless discipline, but they weren't accustomed to others, especially what appeared to be bikers, so relishing in dispatching violence.

Smitts approached the stage, chin raised and unflinching. Joe raised a hand to warn him about the scannerbots, but even as Smitts ascended the steps, the machines' guns remained silent, if at the ready.

"Welcome, Mayor Smitts," one of the bots said in its neutral deadpan.

Smitts grinned at the play-on-words.

The bot turned to Joe, "Welcome, Lawman Grissom."

Smitts really got a kick out of the robot, "It works! My God, it *works!*" He looked over his shoulder at his entourage, "I don't know what you all did, but that's a nice touch—thanks. I'll make sure you're suitably 'rewarded' tonight."

Meyer looked up at Joe and placed a hand on his shoulder, "Lawman," he said, before he broke into a broad grin.

Joe widened one eye as his lip twitched, "Thank you, Meyer. 'Preciate what you did for my boy."

Smitts waved him off, "Nothing of it, nothing of it," he patted Joe twice on the shoulder as he leaned in and whispered, "just keep your end of the bargain, now."

Smitts had a bounce in his step as he approached the microphone, with a number of the grungy-looking characters in tow. The one with the cowboy hat walked up to Joe. He hocked up a loogie and spat it on the floor before he held a stinger stick out to Joe.

Joe took the device and attached it to his belt.

Smitts tapped on the mike several times, "People of Starship City, good evening. I know today's been pretty rough on you, so I'll keep this short. The bad news is, *Minerva's* leaving, in just about," he checked his watch, "oh, another minute or so. Your government has abandoned you, and to a patriot like myself, *that* is a horrible tragedy."

He let the words wash over the room for a moment, "However, as the old saying goes, every cloud, and *believe* me, there are about to be a whole *bunch* of those, has a silver lining," he straightened his collar and pointed both thumbs at his chest, "you're lookin' at him. I'm Meyer Smitts, the new Mayor of Starship City. As long as you remain calm and do as you're told, everything will be fine."

Great, Joe thought, *I'm working for a guy who talks like a bank robber.*

"In a few moments, you're going to see a fantastic show, one conceived in the 1960s by President Kennedy's top scientists and advisors. A plan so mocked, so derided back in the day for the damage, outright *carnage* it would do to this planet, that it was shoved into a drawer, and allowed to gather dust for a century."

Joe felt a tap on his shoulder. It was the cowboy again. This time, he held out a pair of thick, dark goggles to Joe.

"What're these for?" Joe hissed.

"Dude, don't you even know what *Minerva* stands for?" the Cowboy asked.

Joe shook his head as he slid the goggles over his head and onto his eyes.

"For now, sit back, relax, enjoy some tasty refreshments that you've gone far too long without, and enjoy!" Smitts motioned to the window as he slid on his own pair of stylish, if thick, sunglasses and turned to face the ship.

A blinding flash of light filled Joe's vision, soaking through the glass. Smitts lit a cigar as a mushroom cloud radiated out from the source of the blast. The room shook violently as an enormous boom rattled the thick, reinforced glass in its panes.

Five seconds later, there was another flash. Then another. Each explosion caused the massive hangar to quake, as bombs continued to go off.

Monsters! Joe thought. *Monsters, all of th—*

He stopped. Through all of the thick clouds, through the winds that swirled outside of the Grand Hall, there was *Minerva*, rising through the air. The enormous ship seemed to defy all known laws of physics as the blasts propelled it upward, through first the sky, then the atmosphere as it ascended toward the heavens.

The cowboy shook his head, "Massive, Interstellar, Nuclear, Engine, Rocket, Vehicle, Application," he said, the words dripping with wonder.

Joe watched with amazement as the blasts continued, well into the unnaturally-purple sky and past. As the ship grew smaller and smaller, so, too did the nuclear explosions as it hurtled into space.

"That's, wow, that's," Smitts paused at the microphone as he turned to face the crowd, "that's something, ain't it, folks?" He applauded briskly into the microphone, echoing what Aguilar mere minutes earlier.

This time, the crowd responded. They set aside their animosity for a few seconds, clapping as their last hope made it into space, and gave them a shot to colonize the stars.

Maybe this won't be such a bad gig after all, Joe thought.

His eyes were drawn to motion in front of the stage. A man grabbed another man and smashed his head into the ground, eyes wild with fear and anger.

Smitts stiffened, as if he took the disruption of order personally. He allowed the fight to continue for several seconds as a thin, conniving grin crept over his face and his gaze turned to Joe.

Joe locked eyes with the man and nodded.

He unbuckled the stinger stick from the clasp on his belt and hit the blue button on its side. Joe stood for a moment, hand outstretched, stinger stick sizzling with activity and took a deep breath. He let the air out and with it let go of who he once was, that weary father who he knew had died moments before.

Joe steeled his jaw, raised his arm, and leapt off the stage, into the fray, swinging, and thinking, all the while.

THANKS FOR READING!

I hope you enjoyed *Rogue*. What started as an idea for a short, 10,000 word or so novelette eventually took on a bit of a life of its own, and became the 23,000 word piece that you just finished. If you liked the story, please feel free to review it wherever you purchased it and/or on Goodreads. Much like the "Powers That Be" of Starship City's claims about the lottery, I'm told that these sites use the reviews as part of their decision of what books to show other folks, so each review can help others find this story in the future. Any help you can provide in that regard is greatly appreciated.

WANT TO FOLLOW MASON AND JOE'S ADVENTURES IN THE FUTURE?

Join D.J.'s mailing list on his website (www.djgelner.com) to be notified when new books are released (complete with a "no spam" guarantee!)

Check Out D.J.'s Other Books:

Jesus Was a Time Traveler

Time travel. Every sober scientist thinks it's utterly impossible.

Of course, Phineas Templeton is no sober scientist in any sense of the word. A quirky English chap with a taste for fine scotch, Dr. Templeton builds a time machine at the behest of his mysterious Benefactor. His mission? To meet Jesus Christ Himself, and garner all of the fame, recognition, and accolades that writing an epic time travelogue would bring.

Unfortunately for Finny, Jesus is actually a fellow time traveler, a hippie named Trent from Colorado. While He explains that the past is fixed and immutable ("What happened, like, *happened*, man..."), Dr. Templeton realizes that he's made a horrible oversight in his calculations, and can't return to his own time period.

The only way home is to follow a list of very specific instructions his Benefactor has hidden on the time machine, which sends him on a madcap, at times hilarious voyage from watching his hero, Sir Isaac Newton, be berated by a high school physics teacher, to hunting dinosaurs, to rescuing two colorful American soldiers and fighting Nazis hellbent on his destruction.

All the while, Phineas is left to question his Benefactor's true intentions. Just who is the shadowy person pulling the strings of a conspiracy thousands of years in the making? And why is Finny so key to their machinations?

A novel that's been called "equal parts *The Da Vinci Code* and *Back to the Future*," *Jesus Was a Time Traveler* is a book that will please fans of Dan Brown and Douglas Adams alike with quirky humor, thought-provoking puzzles, cryptic clues, and a finicky universe that would like nothing more than to keep things as they are.

HERE'S WHAT REVIEWERS ARE SAYING:

"A thoroughly enjoyable novel: equal parts 'Da Vinci Code' & 'Back to the Future' make it a novel you don't want to put down! I thoroughly enjoyed this philosophical--and funny--adventure through the centuries!" -A Merchant Site

"I found the book engrossing. The trip through history and our future was fun to take with the Doc!!" -A Merchant Site

"it made me want to keep turning the page to see what would happen next. It was engaging and I thought the plot was creative and interesting." -Goodreads

(Available in Paperback, Kindle, Nook, iBooks, Kobo, and Smashwords Formats)

Hack: The Complete Game

Roger "Hack" O'Callahan is angry. Even though he's managed four World Series-winning teams over a career spanning more than forty years, he's finally encountered a foe he can't beat: Liver cancer.

Armed with a supply of his favorite cheap whiskey ("Old Reliable") and with his sharp tongue zipping off callous remarks from his foul mouth, Hack decides to spit in the face of his impending demise by worming his way into managing the AA Hoplite Magpies, a team divided and at odds with each other and the rest of the Northern League. As Hack instills a little "old school" discipline in this rag-tag bunch, he comes to find that his players are keeping secrets of their own, shocking secrets that threaten to tear his clubhouse and the world of sports apart at the seams.

A comedy similar to *Major League* or *Bull Durham*, but with several dark twists, the *Hack* trilogy will keep you laughing and guessing until its shocking conclusion.

(Available in Paperback and on Kindle, Nook, iBooks, Kobo, and Smashwords formats)

ABOUT THE AUTHOR

D.J. Gelner is a sportswriter, radio personality, and attorney. He worked at a large law firm for several years before shifting his focus to writing full-time. He lives in Clayton, Missouri with his dog, Sully.